PATRICE

A POEMELLA

PATRICE

A POEMELLA

GERI GALE

Patrice: a poemella
By Geri Gale

Copyright © 2014 by Geri Gale
First edition: February 2014
Please visit www.gerigale.com

ISBN: 978-0-986-05900-1 (Trade Paper)
ISBN: 978-0-986-05901-8 (eBook: EPUB)
ISBN: 978-0-986-05902-5 (eBook: MOBI)

Library of Congress Control Number: 2013918138

Design by Pamela Farrington.
Cover design by Pamela Farrington.
Proofreading by Anne Moreau.

Printed in the United States of America.

PK & Alex Co.
4616 25th Avenue NE #363
Seattle, WA 98105

Printed on recycled acid-free paper.

For
Patricia E. Gale
&
Patty Kunitsugu aka PK

poemella \pō-'me-lə\ n. 1 : a literary narrative that is part poem and part novella 2 : written by a woman 3 : composition possesses the inherent qualities of the sweet richness found in fruit 4 : consists of four themes connected through a sequence of images, emotions, and external events: art, love, war, and timelessness

She would not say of any one in the world now that they were this or were
that. She felt very young; at the same time unspeakably aged. She sliced like a
knife through everything; at the same time was outside, looking on. She had
a perpetual sense, as she watched the taxi cabs, of being out, out, far out to sea
and alone; she always had the feeling that it was very, very dangerous to live
even one day. Not that she thought herself clever, or much out of the ordinary.

—Virginia Woolf, *Mrs. Dalloway*

The solace of such work as I do with brain and heart lies in this—that only
there, in the silences of the painter or the writer can reality be reordered,
reworked and made to show its significant side. Our common actions in
reality are simply the sackcloth covering which hides the cloth-of-gold—the
meaning of the pattern. For us artists there waits the joyous compromise
through art with all that wounded or defeated us in daily life; in this way,
not to evade destiny, as the ordinary people try to do, but to fulfil it in its true
potential—the imagination.

—Lawrence Durrell, *Justine*

BOOK ONE

Summer

1. Summer 1939

LOUIS IS A SUFFERING SOUL. EXCEPT FOR HIS LOVER HADRIAN, ALL HE HAS
EVER LOVED HAS DIED. HIS FAMILY AND FRIENDS WERE TAKEN IN A TRAIN TO
BUCHENWALD AND RAVENSBRÜCK, AND HE WAS SMUGGLED OUT OF VIENNA
IN A COFFIN. HE LIVES IN EXILE IN THE CITY AND DREAMS OF PAINTINGS AND
MYSTERY AND THE SPLENDORS OF DEATH.

He stood slumbrous in a remote corner of the city, facing his art.
The day changed and repostured itself as his mother looking
in the evening mirror clasping a ruby necklace around her birdlike neck.
A tall and gallant grandfather clock breathed, witnessed the painter's
small hours. A stained glass of red wine on the fireplace mantel
was flecked with leftover intimacy the painter had shared hours before
with his lover Hadrian who had doused his body with kisses,
the way pain pulls when it endures too long.

Moments passed and twilight burned the city. Twilight rippled,
careened charmed hues over the canvas, soaked his painting
with the magnificent dust of dusk. He moistened his lips with his tongue
and lifted the Viennese paintbrush in his left hand. The darkest color
of red stuck to the bristles. The powers over him watched and waited
for the painter to begin, breathed night's captive ardor on his flesh,
a seductive scent he loathed in the summer of his discontent.

Night emasculated day. Night came and robbed him of his sun.
Night pilfered his strength. The canvas held his passion. His blemishes
now hidden by the disappearance of light, and yet failure weighed
heavy in his bones. The paintbrush grew limp in his hand.

His eyes searched for meaning under and around the woman's anatomy.
Somewhere in the distance incense was lit, intoxicated smells roamed
night avenues of money and love, red meat sizzled.
Somewhere in the distance, orthodox men sipped dark coffee
and spoke a secret language, memorized code
partitioned to the dispossessed in small amounts.

He closed his eyes and ran his palm along her contours, her curves.
He remembered the soft texture he had embedded in her
during the early morning hours when he was androgynously sane.

Now the dry, hardened ridges of her landscape dug at his skin.
He tightened his veins as if he were standing before a noble hurt animal.

The grey corset he had laced with the finest
lines imaginable radiated iron-silver.
The kept woman confined night's rupture
in the stays of her harnessed heart.

Night confused him. Night savaged him. Night shadowed her face.
A live creature came to life. Her lips broke into an awkward smile.

A puff of wind invaded the harbor. The windows rattled. He slung his eyes
away from her and he looked out toward the horizontal city.
The roar of the river and the thunder of the wind unraveled his loneliness.
The Brooklyn Bridge rose from the river like dusk-silver lusterless animal
flesh, resurrected from the splendors of death.
Nothing could be more free, to die and to be reborn.

He pressed his forehead against the unsteady glass and bent to his knees
on the hardwood floor and studied his own face in night's dark mirror.
The amount of time it takes to unearth a masterpiece of art
hammered at his spine.
His paintbrush touched the glass.
The glass quaked with wind.
He gasped for air, steadied his wrist.
He feathered a sea of black on the glass.
He traced the geometry of the bridge.
Out of the corner of his eye he saw a black barren mass.
He dabbed the alchemy of his paint into the black sac.
Every thought in him resisted the temptation to burrow his venom inside.
His disenchantment of self stretched silken lines from the orb,
upward and downward, toward and away.
He drew lines. He angled them. He bridged and framed them.
He connected them. He spun and spun small quantities of empty
space at breathless speeds.
A centric pattern formed. Spokes from a common origin.
All primitive life suffused in him, everything that mattered, mapped
order out of chaos.
Every small atom in him freed marrow and bone.
Every part of him longed to preserve the early childhood

memory of spider-black and morning dew clinging to gossamer threads.
He peeled the paintbrush from the glass.
The spider and her web, safe from danger, clung to the glass.

The grandfather clock chimed night ten times. He stood to his feet
and admired the window sketch. He cleaned his brush. He smelled
the oil, inhaled minerals. He carried the turpentine-soaked rag to
his mouth, saturated his mouth with the acrid scent of the day's work.
He was incendiary with fumes, if he were to light a match for another
cigarette he would burn. Time pissed and pissed away as the painter
held to his vision of the world to come.

His dead grandfather's voice. "Louis, I am a clockmaker. Be a painter
if you must. Be careful, very careful. Creation was given to humans
not angels. By leaving out or adding one color, you may destroy the entire
world. Leave Vienna in this coffin and never return. The clock is in this
other coffin. Life is full of our inability to imagine the outcome. Always
remember the time these hungry men in the sickly intestines of one black
stallion entered and slaughtered our city in surprise. Drink to life.
Get drunk on life. Paint only what you want remembered."

And then, although the painter was alone in the room, he felt his
grandfather's palsied hand shake his shoulders. As if an invisible hand
held him tight, he felt the bone of his grandfather's fingers and the
imprint of his wounds. His heart pounded with excitement. Bony fingers
clenched his neck, and the rag fell violently from his mouth.

2. Summer 1939

PATRICE IS TIRED OF BEING IMMORTAL. SHE IS WEARY OF BEING REPRESENTED
AS AN OBJECT OF BEAUTY. SHE LONGS TO RELEASE HER SECRETS AND ESCAPE
HER FIVE-HUNDRED-YEAR-OLD LIFE. EVERY TEN YEARS SHE TRAVELS TO A NEW
CITY TO POSE NUDE ON A RED VELVET COUCH FOR A PAINTER, INFUSING HIM
WITH PASSION TO UNLEASH HIS ART.

In the morning, an arc of white the shape of a woman's eyelash hung
over the city. She stood on the precipice of time looking into the distance.
The mythology of the city lured. Summer's opiate of dead souls sifted
through her wax bones. Memories like butterfly wings tormented her
smooth skin with small hours of existence.

A murder of crows flew over her.
Black wings blotted out the sky.
She stood buried in thought and smelled
the foul stench of dead fish,
the trace of oil, the scent of humans.

The Brooklyn Bridge shaped like a prehistoric animal rising from sleep,
glistened masculine strength. She shuddered. Her shoulders bent.
She inhaled her own wind in the pit of her throat. She made herself wild and
large. She kicked off her shoes as though she could gallop across the bridge,
tossing her gorgeous mane like an unbridled mare entering the city.

Time hammered the harbor.
Plates of land shifted underneath.
She heard the tyranny of voices.
Harsh cries of the wind relentlessly crashed.

The thunderous angry roar of the East River rushed under her, shackling
waves, cracking branches and smashing rocks, spawning back to the dark
forest floor. She heard captive ships slaved to the berth, ropes slipped and
tied, chains cinched, rusted anchors weighted down, the countenance of
ships waiting and waiting to unleash their bodies from land.
Her skin secreted tears.

The gates of New York City opened and the city's obsessive rhythms came
to life. The going and coming moved swiftly while the gravity of earth held

her steady and composed in a compassed direction as she walked the streets
alone, cautious, careful not to live too much of life, not to breathe in the
communal air of a civilization so close to danger and pallor of disgrace.

A stranger among strangers, she walked and walked the streets, and she felt
a gathering around her, the satiated pleasure of movement beside her,
and for a moment she neglected her purpose and forgot the veined venomous
history splintered on the streets. She stopped walking and a sudden summer
breeze like an opulent tongue reminded her of her hunger.
She tasted the frailties and feasted on the stealing hours.

The morning sun spilled on her olive skin.
Her bare shoulders trickled warmth.
Light shone on her face, blinded her eyes.
Her smouldering eyes welcomed the sun.
The touch of sun melted her heart, stripped her of darkness,
emblazoned her with brilliance, flattered her with independence.
Nothing could penetrate her except for the sun.
Nothing could harm or destroy her.

She admired her own reflection in the brittle window glass.
Her black and yellow dress hung shapely. She was both beautiful
and horrible. She saw her strength and her helplessness. She saw
eyes that witnessed her corrupted and polluted beauty betrayed
and fermented in deception.
Eyes of men preened her skin for tissued lust of flesh.
Yellow sadness and blue madness pricked at her skull.
The city breathed apparitions. She heard the words of women
fondling trust, salivating the lyrics of a sea of birds, unseen,
but heard, invisible, but heard, heartbeats thrumming the bitterness
of an empty womb, each step, each gesture embedded with fallen
petals of dead souls, buried bodies, and ashes of bones.
An ever-growing look of horror shadowed her face.

And then, she heard peals of laughter and she smelled sweet perfume,
so strong, so purple, so explicit in its promise of delivery from the past,
from all that she had carried with her into this new time.
She turned and left her reflection on fragile glass for others to admire
and dream all things that are to come, and she ceremoniously walked
untroubled to the painter, in the vein of giving.

3. Summer 1939

WHAT ALWAYS HAPPENED, THEN HAPPENED. IT CAME TO PASS THEY WERE
KEPT APART UNTIL THE FINEST HOUR OF THE DAY WHEN THE NATURE
INHERENTLY IN THE WOMAN AND IN THE MAN DREW THEM TOGETHER AT
THE WHITE RABBIT CAFÉ.

A summer too hot to breathe, the terrible tendrils of sun penetrated
the fabric of the painter's white shirt and black pants and pricked at his flesh,
his skin the yellow-stained color of an old stamp hidden in a drawer
that had not seen sun in years.

He looked at the skyline, a panorama of civilization frothed with
consumption and slick with greed. He lived in a city of exiles where
foreigners come to suck blood. He smelled steel and tar and nets
of captured fish. The city made love with fate. He looked toward the river
and studied the slight sway of a red flag tied to the mast of *Queen Mary*
and he breathed in night's leftovers, night's lovemaking in her galley and
stern. He walked away from water, and he followed strolling men traveling
in clusters and alone, lovely sane men who learned to saunter like women
along paved streets.

He dreamed of greatness. He dreamed of leaving a trail of his existence.
He dreamed of the possibility of chance. After night's somber onslaught,
he longed for the rarity of a new day. He stopped at a warehouse window
and admired a sculpture of a woman. Her hands gloved, crystal beads
sewed to white porcelain cloth like stitches to the flesh of slim wrists.
Transformation of white.
His eyes were drawn downward to her delicious flaw.
Bare feet and the little toe, not cut off, but mangled.

He turned the same corner. Never had the White Rabbit Café
looked so emblazoned and austere. Minnows of light blistered along
the façade the way beads of sweat stream down the flesh when
two lovers depart after time spent together. The desert-gold door
was closed, sealed like a tomb, the brass doorknob unpolished
with the marks of a thousand hands opening a door to intoxicated
bliss, opening a world where waiters served men drinks and food,
filled men with dreams, with imaginary women, drowned them
with vodka and wine, fattened them with sugar and cream.

Four and a half hours into his day, he sat at his table in the westerly corner.
His table was set. His chair wiped clean. He smelled clean clothes pressed
with slaved hands, polished leather shoes, the scent of bottled cologne,
combed hair, and the hungered madness of questing for unattended love.
People floated by from the past to the future like secrets one receives.

"Your view perfectly arranged like a movie. The corner represents the entirety
of New York. The Brooklyn Bridge peaks in the horizon for the painter,"
Hadrian had said.

Louis the painter ran his thin featherlike hand through his black curls.
The man sitting next to Louis chewed on ice, the sound of a sculptor
carving on a hot summer day.
Louis held the yellow pencil in his left hand, the weight of his instrument
lofty as a quill.
Light splattered the tabletop and sliced his hand in half.
His hand became warm and soft. He licked the nib.
The lead sweet and delicious tasted like the blood of plums.
He pressed his spine against the black cast-iron rungs of the chair.
He imagined the woman in the warehouse window now naked
as he imagined the sculptor had conceived her, as most artists began
at the beginning, stripped bare.

His habit began.
His first mark on the blank page dim.
"Kill your memory and you will learn how to paint," Franz had said.
His erect pencil swept across the page. Not the sun, nor the terrible heat,
nor trust that evaporated, nothing could stop the pencil from moving.
Art tormented the yellow lead tongue. Shadows could be made
to speak and scream.
He attached hands to arms with the blackest black he mastered with lead,
a trick taught to him by Franz, one he vowed never to share with another.
Franz's relationship with black. Out of darkness comes white.
He secretly drew seven veins, a number embedded for those who came
to the portrait looking for something else, a secret formula
only the desperate solve.

Dark-armed Hadrian Salvino stood at the mahogany bar and stared
at the painter. The pallor of Hadrian's sad mouth. Lips tight at the corners.
His testicles tight. Black pants tight at the seams. Elbows extended out
like hunted bones pinned tight to a wall.

His eyes moved to the onyx-marbled eyes embedded in the floor.
Hadrian had watched the sculptor conceive her. The old man had knelt
on the floor. He had begun with pure, absolute white as though it were
only natural for an artist on his knees to begin his creation with the color
of snow, for it was cold, the way the patrons watched over him.
The sculptor had dipped his fingers into water and sprinkled the small tiles
as if cleansing the foreheads of sinners. Hadrian had watched the sculptor's
hollowed armpits swell with the tears of yesterday's years, the cruel hands
of time roiling down his dry withered skin along his ribs. The sculptor had
formed the shape of a magician's white rabbit wearing a black top hat.
He chiseled pink feet and murmured, "Mon ami. Mon ami. You mean
more to me than humans."
He spat in the mortared mixture of sand and water in the way Hadrian's
grandmother spat at the ubiquitous evil eye as fortune and freedom
slipped through her Sicilian fingers and Moroccan feet.

Hadrian approached the painter's table with the quietness of a cat.
He looked down at the drawing and whispered, "Louis, I thought you
might not come."
The patrons at the table in the northern corner shouted, "Draw me.
Draw me. Not him."
Hadrian's lips smiled. He knew Louis would never draw the imperfect,
flawed body of a man.

The woman opened the door. As it is when something quite out of the
ordinary happens, time came to a standstill. Conversation stopped.
Drunken silence filled the White Rabbit Café. Her bare shoulders framed in the
doorway under harsh light radiated a halo stricken with summer's enormity.
Her hair loosened and fell to her sleeveless shoulders. She moved a lock of

hair off her face and searched through the cloud of men and smoke and
awakened the consciousness that lay dormant in the heart of everyone.
"I am still alive," her lips moved, but she was not heard.

Louis studied her entrance at the front door from afar. He saw her body
full of mystery and suffering. His mind peppered elation. Her alarming beauty.
Her face, the eyes of a woman who has learned the secrets of the grave,
her skin like a fragment of lost civilization, a broken piece
from a hand-painted vase.
Her impossible lasting beauty.
His body ached for her tranquility.

Hadrian stood, his elbows digging into the mahogany bar, and he watched
Louis watch this woman. Hadrian pried his elbows from the bar,
making the sound of rusty nails dug from wood, and he ushered the woman
to a faraway corner in the east side of the café.

The rabbit's black glass-marbled eyes stared at her with the piercing mockery
of the make-believe. She stepped over the white rabbit and tempered herself
to the canon of memory, to the branch-rivered tempest of truth she carried
in the underflesh of her arm.
She sat across from Louis and held herself in a fine moment
when time is stayed and reined with the exacting strength
of a queen bee among drones.

"Who is she?" Louis asked.
"I've never seen her before," Hadrian said.
"Bring her a glass of red wine from me."
"Are you sure? Let's wait for the next one."
"This is the one. There will never be another one like this."
"She will destroy you."
"She's the one we've been waiting for. We have nothing to fear.
Such a beautiful and sublime being can bring me no harm."

Hadrian delivered a glass of red wine to the woman's table.
"A gift from the man in the corner."
"I don't take gifts from strangers."
"He's not a stranger. He is a painter."
She smiled, offered a toast in the air, raised the glass to her lips
and took a long, drawn-out sip. "Thank him for me. Would you please?"

She traced little patterns with her finger on the glass.
"He has money."
"Do I look like a woman who needs money?" She smelled her dead brother
in the room. She sensed the waiter had served him, fattened him with
women and wine and cream.
"Everyone here needs money."
"He is an artist. He must be poor."
"His family sent him away."
"Sent him away?"
"Sent him away with enough to buy you and a hundred like you."
Her delicate hand formed a fist around his wrist. "There is only one like me.
Take me to him and then leave."

She stood in silence and looked down. She brushed her hand over
the pencil drawing.
She kneeled to the floor and lifted the painter's chin in her hands.
She wrenched her will to his.
"You master her, but you do not master the art."
"It is my nature. I cannot help myself."
"Others have painted me, what makes you different?"
"I will do anything you ask. All artists give up something when
they paint. I will give you everything, everything, everything."
"Why must the conversation with a woman always begin with a lie?"
"The beginning is fantasy. The test of our relationship is time.
Give me time and you will be pleased with the outcome."
"I fear you have no fighting strength left inside."
Neither said a word for a while.

She raised herself and stood behind him. She blew cool air onto his neck.
"Let me tell you about tomorrow," she said. "My name is Patrice.
I will come to you in the morning."

4. Summer 1939

BEGIN DAY, WHEN RUIN AND RELENTLESS STRIFE SUBSIDED IN THE CITY'S WILDERNESS AND WASTES, IN THE MONTH OF AUGUST, IN THE YEAR NINETEEN HUNDRED THIRTY-NINE, WHEN THE WOMAN AND THE MAN BEGAN THE FIRST, THE FIRST, THEIR FIRST DAY OF LABORIOUS WORK.

She walked unhurried. Her footsteps echoed like loving accomplices.
There was no limit to the city hues. Hoary bare shoulders, copper eyes,
bronze split lips, the glow of heavenly bodies watching overhead.
Summer, a city in full bloom. The prologue of doom. Silver-lined shoes.
The city streets' golden tooth. Once a blue moon. Too much to worship
yet nothing to tend.

The news of Patrice's arrival crawled mouth-to-mouth up The Metropolitan's
stairs. They sang to a woman wearing a black and yellow dress. They sang to
a woman climbing the stairs with an uncensored look of a fulfilled life.
They sang taller than the painter. More lustrous, more splendid, more
resilient than the painter. No jewelry on her skin. Nothing in her hands.
They sang and sang to the most ravishing one ever to enter the building.

Patrice stood still for a moment on the threshold.
She looked at the grand height of the vaulted ceiling and the aged hardwood
floor. The room spilled morning light from three tall windows.
She saw a grandfather clock, a distinguished antique that did not belong
standing deathless side by side so many different relics of modern time.
She saw in the corner a three-legged easel, and on a table there were
purple irises abloom in a glass vase and fingerprinted tubes of paint lined
precisely in a row, and in the center of the room she saw a red velvet couch
with elegant lion's paws, and on the walls she saw paintings of women,
a landscape of violets, blues, and greys, bodily skies turning into watery
luscious grapes.
She saw the painter waiting nervously with a cigarette burning, standing
in a room with a history, where lovers were born, where lovers died, a room
that could no longer be cleansed for the aroma lingered like a plague of an
artist in search of the perfect red, and she stood fixed with a pulsing rush of
longing for her first portrait to be painted in deep, crimson scarlet-fever red.
Although in the room there was nothing to be afraid of—
Patrice shrank at the sight.
A rare sensation invaded her. Her limbs weakened.

She stood in the doorway at a loss, vulnerable and fragile,
face to face with something which so far had never existed.

She trembled a break in her breath, a slim breath of life leaving her.
She recoiled, lost her nerve, stepped back and braced her body against the
doorframe, held herself against the wood to preserve the life still in her.
A blaze of fire seared through her heart. She let out a sigh.
The painter held out a hand to her. "Should I carry you across the threshold?"
In his left hand Patrice saw something she had never seen in other hands,
and she sprang back with an insurgence of faith.
"Nothing harmful except art ever happens in The Metropolitan."
Louis lowered his arm.
Her moist dress clung to her flesh.
She cleared her throat and said in a calm voice,
"I met a lovely woman on the stairs. Mrs. Ito told me to tell you to act as if . . .
as if you were an heir to the gift of this day."

Their first conversation in the room: The dreadful hot weather.
If rain did not fall soon the city might burn. Even bricks, iron, and steel
needed water to survive this hell.
They turned from each other and found themselves in a shy moment,
both staring at the black spider and her web painted on the glass, both
sneaking a delicious peek of the Brooklyn Bridge windowscape.

She slipped out of her black leather heels. She unbuttoned her dress.
It slid quietly past her thighs, her patellae, to her toes.
She stood barefooted in a pool of wet black and yellow cloth.
A breeze from the open windows passed over her breasts.
She listened to the breath of the painter, to the memory of the breath
of the Russian patriarch who forced her to eat blindfolded, cloth draped
over her eyes to induce his sexual appetite. She remembered his words:
Only men know how to paint.
"Now what?" Patrice asked.
Louis pointed. "Over there."

She lifted a red pillow and smelled the velvet. She smelled a lineage
of other women who had lain on the couch. She smelled gardenias
and rosemary and lost hope. She smelled sugar, the sea, and torn dreams.
She smelled broken bones, bruised arms, and lonesomeness.
She sank into the couch. She lay like a corpse, her back pressed to the red
velvet, her arms crossed over her chest, her body a stone in water, sinking.
Her eyelids, closed petals, quivered. She arched her neck, and memory
spilled and trilled with the spirits of the wild as souls do when they return
from the dead.

Franz appeared and watched her every move. She sensed his curiosity.
How Louis's painting teacher Franz coursed through his dead brain to find
her existence on an old classical page, how he searched his memory for
knowledge of her from museums he had devoured during his youthful years
as an art student in Vienna, Paris, Madrid, and Rome.
Franz told her how he had urged Louis with encouraging words, berated
him only for his mistakes, and showered him with praise when he chose
the most brilliant color to resuscitate the recessed dying landscape.

Franz was an intelligent man, he was named in the spirit of dispelling myth.
Patrice taught him language in a few words. He was desirous to learn.
Wary of a woman's voice. Superstitious and afraid of a woman's touch.
She told him to go away. He refused to leave. She warned him he stood
in the way. "You and your pride. You are a jealous old man. You never loved
him. You only wished to possess him. If you do not fly away, his art will die.
The old must be discarded for the new. Only a woman can teach him
about the unexplored. Men have done all they can do."
"I shall return," he said.

She touched her hips, ran her palms underneath her chilled legs for warmth.
"Place your hands where I can see them," Louis said.
"Men are the slaughterers of the earth." She licked her lips and opened
her eyes.
"Yes, but please do keep still."

Louis kept himself closeted in darkness at a sentimental, safe distance
behind the canvas in the corner across the room.
Patrice's neck cried out for a string of rubies, as if there were only one
necklace in the world, the one he clasped around his mother's neck
as she sat on the bench before the vanity mirror and admired herself
and her son on their last day.
Blue inched out from the tube in a continuous snakelike strand,
magnesium-blue begging, asking to be fanned over yellow and on top of red,
to dab the first painting of Patrice with water and sky, courting him to infuse
the deepest sorrow with wings of youth, waxing him with the scent
of sapphire bliss, the cruel, cruel color of blue, of blue misgivings
and blue loss.

He painted Patrice first in cubes, geometric squares, tiny blue coffins
he stippled with silver nails. He added white. Blue edges turned
into sails, her body a harbor of white cloth blowing in the wind,
charting its uncompassed course.

One hour later, when he painted her red, she could hear the melancholy
of his bristles, the sweeping of animal hairs as if his palm swirled along
her neck. She could hear him paint her flesh the color of clay, the skin
of a chestnut, smooth and concealed. She heard his stomach hungering
for more, for more red meat and potatoes and red wine.
Her heartbeat quickened when he painted her breasts,
she rode a white mare panting through the woods,
her torso perched above clouds.
At the edge of the woods she saw a woman with violin in hand,
the strings of the bow arched, a breast removed.
Patrice placed her palm on her warm belly and watched it rise.

A pigeon came on the fire escape for her morning food. Louis opened
the window and palmed her a piece of bread. His finger touched
her belly and she flew away. He turned from the window and said,
"When my paintings of you hang in the museum she will accept a kiss."

Patrice planned her outfit. She imagined attending the opening
together, her body draped like beautiful linen on his arm.
"How long will it take?" she asked.
"Art takes unswerving hours of trust."
"The last painter hurt me. Birds fly away when hurt. I wanted to stay
but I could not."

At lunch he served her bread and butter and wine. He took a cantaloupe
in his hands as though he held a globe of the world. He turned it round
and round and cut it in half in one violent slice. The two sides fell
to the table and rocked back and forth. He took a spoon and scooped
out the seeds, then carved out the meat. Juice overflowed onto the table,
spreading in all directions through the cracks to the hardwood floor.
Cantaloupe juice dripped on Patrice's toes. The smell of fruit was sweet
and fresh, and the room became a bowl of fruit. She leaned forward,
opened her mouth. He did not move. She lifted her body off the ladder-back
chair. He made her beg for her reward. The melon in her mouth turned into
summer, she a child sucking on the heat and the sun, her first summer
she gives up milk, turns to fruit, cannot get enough.

A young girl played the piano at three o'clock and the traffic outside
increased and Patrice lay on the couch and listened, feeling the subway
quaking underneath.
A mother's voice downstairs demanded her daughter play her piano more.
The sacrifices I made for you, she cried at the young girl.

Cooing of pigeons lured and cajoled, and Patrice broadened her chest
toward the ceiling. "My mother once was a musician. She married instead.
I was not allowed to play the piano in front of my mother. I was expected
to pretend the piano did not exist. It was a dead world, the lack of music
in my father's home." She took a sip of red wine, ran her tongue along
her lips and closed her eyes. "If she had not been excluded. If she had
been invited in . . ."

Louis listened to her breathe. How easily she slept, how quickly
she submerged herself into dream.
He walked to the couch, bent to the hardwood floor.
His knees cracked. He smelled the wine settled in her throat.
He longed for her to leave now that he had found her, for she lay
different from the other women who had lain on his couch.
She lay uncaptured and free.
He moved a stray hair off her face, then slowly returned to his corner.

In the first painting of Patrice, he formed the bristles into a spear
and planted a seed in a fold of the white sail. Its sex unknown. He dipped
his paintbrush in black and began with a box. Thin legs held the heavy weight.
He outlined a black shiny Steinway piano.
He twirled the paintbrush between his thumb and index finger, and he broke
the white sac with the tip of the wood handle. Water gushed from skin.
Red blood marbled across the canvas.
The seed turned into a girl. Small breasts, birdlike neck, long curly brown hair.
Shoulders bent, small limp hands hung through a hole in her lap.
Her mouth motionless. Lavender eyes purred. He lifted the young girl
and placed her on wood stairs. The pitch of the stairs unnaturally high.
The angle of the stairs perversely wide. A banister carved with serpents hissing.
The young girl raised her hands to her ears to shut out daybreak noise.
He painted the sound of water running. Her mother outside in the garden.
The sound of her mother cutting stems of flowers with stainless-steel scissors.
The mother placed the irises in a glass vase, gifts she offered to her piano
she refused to play, but admired each day. The mother looked into a silver mirror.
The young girl watched her mother looking in the mirror, saw the musician
her mother would have become if only she had not been forced to marry
the young girl's father, a man she did not love.
He thickened the mother's legs. Sparkled her brown eyes with gold.
Slipped her feet into black high heels. Hands pressed to her throat,
fingers laced. Her slender piano hands strangled her neck.
He covered the silver mirror with a black cloth. Walked her to the piano.
She carried the vase. Eyes closed. She dreamed of burning the piano,
lighting a match and listening to the black and white keys weeping
a trilogy song. She ran her palm along the piano as if touching the back
of a black seal. A live animal beached. A live animal stranded in a foreign

*place where it did not belong. The piano, a gift delivered from her husband
sent to torment her and remind her of her artistic past.
He painted her fingers longer. He gave her deep crimson, scarlet-fever
red veins. Her hands hovered over the black and white keys
like painted red and purple butterflies in Mrs. Ito's Japanese fan.
Her hands fluttered like untethered wings. He lowered the mother
down to the piano bench. Her back faced the world. Her bare feet
stretched and pressed down on brass pedals. Her spine bent down
toward the onyx-black and ivory-white keys, and the flowers in the vase,
the iris petals fell one by one to the shiny black surface as the mother
pressed her ears to the keys. The young girl's hands moved from her ears
to her thighs. He unfurled her rigid body and her limber back sprawled
across the wood stairs as Mozart waved along her spine.*

Patrice turned her body away from him and asked, "Are you done?"
He covered her body with his blue terrycloth robe.
"Are you pleased?"
He busied himself with his hands. He tucked her in. The robe covered
every inch of her flesh, except her face. He combed her hair with his fingers.
"It is time for me to leave." She pushed him away.
"I must leave before it turns dark."
"I will walk you home."
"No, I will be safe."
He watched her dress. "Perhaps you would like one more glass
of Hadrian's wine before you leave?"
"One glass is the perfect amount."
"Will you come back to me tomorrow?"
"I will come."
"Do you promise?"
"I promise." She covered the painter's lips with her moist palm.
"But tonight you must promise to forget me."

5. FALL 1939

AND SO SHE RETURNED AS PROMISED, AND THEY TOOK THEIR PLEASURE FROM
EACH OTHER EVERY DAY. HE PAINTED HER AS SHE LAY NAKED ON THE RED
VELVET COUCH AND SHE CONTEMPLATED HIS PSYCHE. THE THOUSANDS OF
PAINTINGS OF HER NO LONGER ENTHRALLED HER. SHE WOULD WAIT FOR
DAYS, MONTHS, AND YEARS FOR LOUIS TO UNEARTH HER HIDDEN ESSENCE.
IF NEED BE, SHE WOULD WAIT A DECADE FOR LOUIS TO UNMINE THE POETIC
IMAGE SHE CONCEIVED FOR HERSELF. SHE PRETENDED AND BEGGED TO LOOK
AT HIS WORKS OF ART, BUT SHE DID NOT NEED TO LOOK AT THE PAINTINGS.
A SEASON PASSED, THE FIRST SUMMER LEFT AND AUTUMN CAME.

He had difficulty in not smiling. She was spread out like a starfish
on the red velvet couch. Her pink-coral flesh smooth and serene,
drawn to the red as if feasting on its threads. If he were to leave
his corner and walk to her world to pry her from her dunes,
he would be unable to perform such a feat for she held herself
to the fabric as if she were guarding her eggs.

And so Louis was taught to leave such women alone, to keep to himself
and pretend he was invisible as they formed their bodies and their minds
in a placid state.
And so he held his paintbrush in his hands with honorable forgiveness,
for his past mistakes and his future forgivings.

He hoarded the cerulean blue for these Scorpion days, for the livelihood
he needed to sustain the serious vision.

In the second painting of Patrice, Louis positioned her in his father's court,
the one perfect sea-nymph among a harem. He shaded the interior
with an impromptu air of grandeur and riches.
He kneeled her at his father's feet, with her hand on his thigh.
Her robed body swung toward the open window like a bowl
of bountiful autumn fruit. He suffused demons. He laid her ear
against his father's hand, as though drawing her into conversation
with his father's devilish greed and murderous conviction.
A sea of cerulean blue forked and divided the good from the bad,
and a host of angels flew overhead to witness the marriage
of father to his son's muse. He speckled thousands of white eggs
in a fertile ribboned heavenly sea, as if birthing a future.

The legs of the easel were a half-inch off the black marks painted on
the hardwood floor. His heart raced for the hour when she stretched her
spine and gasped for air, and she would rise from the couch and tiptoe
to the window to catch a glimpse of the fountain of nymphs in the courtyard,
and he would cover the painting with the black cloth. The portrait was never
his to own, yet he could not stop himself from possession, and he could not
permit her to look at herself because of his own unlucky superstitions.

The birds outside his window begging for bread on the fire escape
reminded him of his father's cruel hand, that outstretched limb so quick
to hurt and inflict fear on his entire being, but she was special, yes she was,
her starfish existence swelled in the room, a waterwave, wave after wave,
and the painting held all the magic of her conversation with his father,
a cerulean blue ribbon of sorrowful heart-wretchedness
in the elusive essential evolution of the lunar autumn paints,
his hand-swiped gesture of fatherly interpretation.

She rose from the couch, and inched behind him and placed her hand
on the small of his back and breathed into the nape of his neck.
His smile spread from his lips to his penis.
She reached out to unveil the black cloth.
He flung his paintbrush like an arrow across the room.
Her wrist turned limp and she let go of the black cloth that draped
the painting from her eyes.

"You let Hadrian and Mrs. Ito look. Why not me?" she asked in a pained voice.
"I'm painting you, not them. Hadrian looks because he sells my paintings.
His father was a painter and he understands the nasty business of art.
Hadrian orchestrated my escape from Vienna. He bribed the officers
and saved me and my grandfather's clock. Mrs. Ito is a nurse,
and she keeps me alive. Her husband is a poet and was drafted
as a Japanese interpreter and is stationed at an army base in Hawaii.
They are all I have left."
"And me?"
"You. If you look, you might leave me, and I would disintegrate."

6. WINTER 1939

EVEN IN THE COLD OF WINTER, PATRICE TRAIPSED THROUGH THE DESOLATE CITY TO THE METROPOLITAN TO BE WITH THE PAINTER. THE METROPOLITAN WAS A PLACE WHERE RULES NEVER CHANGED. THERE WERE FEW INTERRUPTIONS OR VISITORS, ONLY RECORDS HE PLAYED OF BACH AND BEETHOVEN AND MOZART AND WAGNER, ONLY HADRIAN AND MRS. ITO. PATRICE AND LOUIS WITHDREW THEIR ATTENTION FROM THE EXTERNAL WORLD TO ENTERTAIN THE MEANINGFUL TRUTH THAT ABIDED IN THE ORNAMENTAL INTERNAL WORLD.

She entered the room carrying a masculine scent. He inhaled the conquering glory of it and watched her undress with the motions of slow deliberateness he had seen in other men, who even when naked kept the most hidden parts to themselves. The joints in his hands ached with the desire to capture the naïveté she wore on her face, that sly look of night's marvels still drenched on her morning flesh. It was an extraordinary December morning, the city shined her citadels of strength, kisses of glass spawned a new beginning of biting cold that would last throughout the day.

She lay on the red velvet couch. Her neck elongated, her hands crossed at her chest and she whispered a line of words she kept to herself as she had done through November, and he knew would continue until the new year for they were at war—in conquest of each other's thoughts like the queen's explorers sent to the new world to wrest the earth's undiscovered riches and spices and spoils.

Her smell lingered in his throat as his paintbrush loitered in the northernmost corner of the canvas. Continents of black gave him a philosophical calm, a sense of lightheartedness he spread with ivory white forming elephant-grey curls of infiniteness, for their first war was near. He was as certain of it as her manliness scrawled across her cheeks, the sun's rays sketching streaks of sword-silver blades he saw in December's deceptive mirth, in the promise of snow they both desired.

Her lips parted, and he witnessed his mistakes in the entangled branches of her hair. The wheel of curls spun away from her bones, and he studied the negative space so anxious for shape. The foundation of her secret lay in the curvature, but her smell reeked of made-up lines,

a madness of reasoning, of making up
and imagining calm in the chaos of battle.

She studied him with a serene introspection, as if looking at him
she looked at herself in a mirror.
He was overcome by desire to know where she had traveled during
the darkest hours of the night, like an insect-lover who claimed,
classified, and named his moth.
Was he painting her alive, her arms white fluttering wings,
or was he doomed to December's cruel hand of cold,
nailing her with pins as he mounted her on a wall?
She watched him smell her, watched how he added more white,
watched his face unveil a look that he wished to fuck her.

He placed his paintbrush down, and he walked to the couch and lifted
her chin in his hands. "Why must you torment me in the winter?"
he asked in the voice of a young schoolboy.

She gasped for air and screamed, "Your hands are ice."
She burst out in laughter, and her once masculine smell turned
sweet and sugary as the breath between them melded into one
cloud of December cold.

He heaved his blood and wrapped his joints into the anatomy of her chin.
His veins let loose, sprawled open, and the pout of her lips
recessed into a crescent-moon smile and she bit him.
She bit his most favorite painting finger, and he dropped to his knees.
His head fell into the cushion of her belly, and for the first time
he knew that his end was near. All along she had teased him
with the scent of a man.

7. *Spring 1940*

IN THE EARLY QUIET MORNING, HADRIAN LEFT WHILE THE OCCUPANTS OF THE METROPOLITAN WERE SOUND ASLEEP. MRS. ITO DELIVERED THE *NEW YORK TIMES* AND SERVED LOUIS COFFEE AND SOFT-BOILED EGGS. BEGINNING IN THE SPRING OF NINETEEN HUNDRED FORTY, PATRICE AND MRS. ITO MET EVERY MORNING ON THE STAIRS AND DISCUSSED MRS. ITO'S DYING HOSPITAL PATIENTS, THE URGENCY OF THE PAINTINGS, THE BOTTLED EMOTIONS OF MEN, AND THE EXCLUSION OF WOMEN PAINTERS FROM THE MODERN MUSEUM. (THE TWO WOMEN NEVER TOLD LOUIS ABOUT THEIR PRIVATE CONVERSATIONS.) PATRICE HAD NEVER SUFFERED LIKE THIS, A DESIRE TO ABANDON THE PAINTINGS AND STAY WITH MRS. ITO ON THE STAIRS.

His eyes boring into her flesh, a groundswell of trembling, a shattered shift from moments before, each hour a transgression, slippage, stoppage, her tranquility stolen, her gracefulness swallowed, his pupils penetrating her being as in the outside world the wind surged, wings like arms pressing against the windowpanes, the all-through-the-ages sound, the captivity pound-pound on glass, his temper rising with each noise, his vision blurred by the interruption of his imperfect gods.

Still she remembered, all great art is an excursion into sorrow and pity.
All great art is an escape from illusion.
Still she remembered, the solace of yesterday's paint, the solitude of the breath between them, the hoary air drifting among them, his vanity prim and proper, his ego swelled like a man amid a secretive affair with a part of his pretend self, the self she gave to Louis in the spring when the grandfather clock wound an elusive chime-charm as if time with the painter would last forever, the spinning of brass gears oiled with spring's saliva.

Patrice yawned, and her fluids shifted deep inside, his eyes still fixed to her breast, the one place he spent the most time, his cushioned resistance, his desire to touch but not to touch, his most favorite part of her body. Her liver no longer held interest, and he had abandoned her heart in winter's foul fall.

A wave rolled from her head to her toes, and his eyes, looking but not listening, remained stationary in the same way she held her mouth open, a test of strength between them as she lay in the field of opposites and he stood in a pool of his own shadow.

Today they were afraid, afraid of each other, the intimacy severed by the
wind, by a force neither one of them could comprehend for they had not
predicted it, nor sensed the fear.
They dismissed it, and abhorred it, and chose to hide it from each other.

But Mrs. Ito sensed it and addressed it on the stairs, and the paintings
of women on the walls, their eyes, too, witnessed the flame, that boring of
one into another, the lack of consent, the tears, the tortured lack of trust.

Her yawn settled in her belly like an echo wail and mouth-to-mouth sparks
flew between them, their universe swelled with the silent exchange of words.
"If you hold still for minutes more, I will behave."
"If you touch me, I will give you the pose of your dreams."

But the women on the walls witnessed the conversation,
deciphered the Morse code—
one short, one long, one part sober and one part question mark, the color
of spring's purple heather blooming his canvas, each stroke more horrific
than the one before, each shadow full of ardor and pity, violet's spectrum
of jealousy clinging to his animal hairs, her shame so thick and dark,
the hide of the paint, her original sin.

Her yawn turned a corner, sleep's call, sleep's promise
of forgetfulness, to sleep and dream her tranquility's return,
to sleep away the eyes of a man.

8. Summer 1940

AFTER LOUIS ATE BREAKFAST, DRANK COFFEE, AND READ THE NEWSPAPER, HE
STOOD AT THE WINDOW AND WAITED FOR PATRICE AND SMOKED A CIGARETTE.
THE RING OF FIRE, A BAND OF CONNECTEDNESS, PULLED HIM FROM NEW YORK
CITY TO VIENNA IN THE SAME WAY A TECTONIC PLATE HELD EARTH'S SURFACE
TOGETHER. A STUDENT OF LIGHT MOVING WITH THE SUMMER SUN, THE DECAY-
ING SMELL OF THE EAST RIVER AND THE LONG SPAN OF THE BROOKLYN BRIDGE
MAGNIFIED THE PAINTER'S REVERIE.

He dreamed for a moment about an isolated quarter of Vienna
that he loved. He looked out The Metropolitan and thought he saw
his mother through the glass as the bus passed by. He felt his mother's
wet hand against his dry skin. She was a well of water when they had
entered the city, a vessel of tears, a sad cushion of resurrection, her flesh
warm and wet, surrounded by strangers on the bus on their way to see Franz.
She had opened her purse and pulled out a white linen handkerchief, had
folded it in tiny precious squares, and then she had unfolded it and held the
wrinkled cloth over her face and it fell from her forehead like a white
parachute with red lipstick stains.
He turned from the window and painted in a leisurely fashion,
reading in the paint whirrs of himself.

In the third painting of Patrice, he divided her hair, bareblue to the east
and bloodred to the west, her curls a current of crested waves swimming
in a sea of troubles. Coated purple bristles hovered over the mounds of her mouth,
the soliloquy of afterlife, the future encrusting the past, each lip the dark side
of the moon, a dark side of love. He stippled his mother's kiss one hundred times,
her mouth the fleshiest and richest place of her face, pockets of minerals
and metallic ores, Venus lips, womanly and manly hungry lips. He beaded
a necklace of rubies cloistered to her neck, clasped her secrets,
her knowledge of passion, the union of his mother's and father's hate,
and he drowned her in an eternal emerald-green sea.
He nippled her breath as she held the pose like a blind woman dictating lost love.
A soft, sexual white linen blew in the wind like a surrendered wedding veil,
and her neck glistened red fertile shells.

The smells and press of human beings came toward him rich with memories
of Franz's studio that he visited as a child with his mother. A dark alley of artists
and whores, painters and poets, musicians and actors and fortune-tellers

mourning loss. A string of animal bones. Fossilized chalk strung like a lantern
across the curtainless windows, the sound of drums, a long-shivering
orgasm of dark, daunted love.

The odor of earth and urine as mother and son slipped through the cracks,
to escape through the evil corridor, to be alone away from his father.
The isolated quarter of Vienna sandwiched between two worlds,
between his grandfather's commissioned clocks hanging
in governmental and religious squares and family clocks standing
in their country home. Mother and son stopped at noon and listened
to his grandfather's chimes, remembering Jewish history at the church
footstool of steepled Christian time.
Inside Franz's studio words were written along the walls, butted
to the ceiling, one long continuous lovepoem scribed, scribbled in black paint
stranded on thirsty walls, a man's love for a married woman,
for Louis's mother who did not belong.
"Lethargic words hang," his mother had said, "poetry should be held
in one's wet hands."

His mother's dry throat and desertlike fingers when near Franz,
but wet with her son, dry beside her cloistered secreted lover
who lived in an isolated part of the city.

Alley shades and guardians whispering, "Go home. Go home."
The beckoning of delicious adult desire, the rank smell
of candlelight burning, turpentine rags soaking in Franz's glass jars,
the sound of rain hammering unrepaired roofs and flooding
tin cans, the allure of cellar ardor descended close to the earth,
the secretive sessions in the studio where Franz taught Louis
how to paint against Louis's father's wishes—a father who believed
there was no money or status in painting, poetry, or art—a civil engineer
who studied and perfected the principles of time by charting
the most efficient way to complete a job in the least amount of time.

Louis dug into his pocket and pressed the white handkerchief
with his fingertips to his palm as if he were a young boy remembering
his mother's red lips pressing the scent of human beings to his palm,
the handkerchief, a white wedding veil like an unforgotten
stretched four-cornered canvas. He removed the white handkerchief
from his pocket and held it to his nose. "She unveiled you to the world

as if you were a piece of art. She wrapped you in the finest blue material.
She invited all to your circumcision, those she liked and all those
who hated her," his grandfather had said.

Louis inhaled the white handkerchief and smelled the city that left
him victorious and vehement in admiration of his mother's vitality,
that left him breathless and resurrected, both alive and dead
when he entered and left.

9. FALL 1940

THE PIGEONS ON THE FIRE ESCAPE OUTSIDE LOUIS'S WINDOW CONGREGATED
IN SILENCE. THE BROOKLYN BRIDGE PEAKED A CHASM. THE WHOLE WORLD
WAS SOMBER AND QUIETLY MOURNING ORDER OF MAGNITUDE LOSS. PATRICE
REACHED FURTHER BACK IN HER MEMORY FOR SOMETHING TO REST ON. OUT
OF NOWHERE THE SOUND OF A HORSE-DRAWN BUGGY REINED PATRICE INTO A
DIFFERENT PLACE, YEARS AGO CROSSING A BRIDGE IN A CARRIAGE. THE PAST AND
THE PRESENT MELDED TOGETHER WITHOUT SEPARATION, A BRAZILIAN DRIVER
FIERCELY WHIPPING THE HORSES AND REFUSING TO SPEAK TO HER FOR HE KNEW
HE WAS CARRYING AN APPARITION, A SWIFT WILD WOMAN FLEEING FROM ONE
PLACE TO ANOTHER, LEAVING LITTLE TRAIL OF HER EXISTENCE.

The shrill of her pose. Patrice was on her knees. She was tired of being
flattened and loved. She was tired of carriages carting away the living
and the dead. She bowed with humility perched on the red velvet.
Waters of sorrows drowned the folds of her thighs. It was a perfect silent day.
The violent wind of yesterday, gone, forsaken like a warrior returned home
to lick his wounds, to contemplate his deep love for those who betray,
the hatred of nations, the conquests of bosses of the earth.

She smelled of rose oil. Her skin illuminated undying particles of scent.
Timid arms stretched out beyond her head, her armpits hollowed
spasms of autumn's near end.
"Why does woman always come back for more violation?" she asked
the painter. Or is the womb a sacrifice? she asked herself.
She bent her neck, and her lips touched and kissed the red velvet with
arrogance. She was not afraid to prostrate herself, to question his desire
to keep her spellbound to her back, she was not afraid to press her buttocks
into the steadfastness of her heels, she was not afraid to bend and shrill.
She removed her lips from the couch and lifted her head.
"The perfect love it comes too late or too soon."
A ray of light cast a pink triangle across her chest.

Traveling and sifting through encrustations of time, she saw he was pious
in his wake, in the refuge of imagination, the paintbrush between his lips
a stick of confession. She saw how Louis looked that day in Vienna
when they carted his mother's limbs away. She saw Louis hidden by his
mother, left behind in the grandfather clock, as rehearsed, Hadrian rescuing
him from the suffocating wood box. She saw Louis's body at the train station

standing in the cloud of steam, his mother's profile, her charcoal face,
Louis's painterly hands gripping his thighs, his guilt, the sound of wheels
grating the steel train tracks, his mother's queenly slim wrist fluttering
and disappearing through steam, each handwave greater than the last.
She saw his mother dressed in biblical blue, rich and deep, sorrowed
bloodletting blue, the train pulling away, his mother's and father's
and grandfather's limbs taken away. His homosexual friends taken away.
She saw Louis's perpetual blissful love for the whole, for dirt and ash and
rubies, for the smell of his paintings burned by Nazis under the birch tree,
for the smell of Max, his great Dane with the one grey-blue eye, devout
and devoted by Louis's side as Louis held his breath in the grandfather clock
box and smelled the land fertilized with his art and his mother's blood.
She saw each brushstroke of paint deeper and richer and more deadly
than the first. Her eyelids quivered. "The way with love, either too late
or too soon," she said out loud.

Dragged back to old, dark places and scenes long-since abandoned,
he obliterated the rubies, once and for all, expunged the memory, the soul
of the ruby. He covered the red with a thick layer of black, night's hand drew
the shades. He unearthed her jewel, cut her throat, hovered in the swallows
of her passionate hell. He unclasped the silver-hooked rectangle he hid
at the nape of her neck. The string of rubies fell to the floor.

Louis was ruined by her love, her sympathy for his art, her desire
to infiltrate his work with her own visionary love of art. He heard
the sound of the beginning—when they first met she had accused
him of siphoning life from a very small room—and he heard and saw
the sound of the end—when they entered her womb and stole her future
nations, the fingerprints of previous thieves who had entered
and departed with her rubies.

The shrill of her voice turned into a deep bass. "Don't you think,"
she asked, "we are taught to love our masters too early in life?"

She bared her teeth. "Your mother. A mother and a son, there is no other
relationship worth painting in your dead room."

Louis returned to her crevices, to her sorrowed strident throat
and stippled grains, grinding her neck to sand.

10. WINTER 1940

THEY WERE A PAIR NOW, A MAN AND A WOMAN, CAPTIVE AND SLAVE, KING AND QUEEN OF SEVEN SEASONS, FEASTING ON THE LAMPSHADE OF ART, HUNGRY AND ANXIOUS FOR PUNISHMENT, FOR THE GREAT LOVE-OBJECT. HER BODY. HIS PAINTS.

In the morning Louis removed the black cloth from the canvas as if lifting
a night shade from a birdcage. Patrice's lips now resonated a beet-red,
night's ardor settled deep in the residue of sleep and dreaminess.
The coldness of her portrait gone. The woodenness of her stature
diminished over time, the way paint grew in the loneliness of the deadly
night. The wind beat against the windows, as the world outside glimpsed her
beauty in an elevated applause, the Americas, New York City, her audience
enraptured by her airs in the gloomy winter morning, dawning
its promise of a new beginning.

He hesitated at first. It was true torture to marvel at his own painting.
It humbled him to saturate himself in praise, how he had calculated
the chemistry of the paint and her desolate mood in the pigments
he had elegantly spread across the landscape of her lips when
she had asked him, "Paint me like you have never painted before."

With tensile strength, he held the paintbrush in his hand and he waited
for her arrival. The wind rattled the windows and then died
as fast as it came.
He wondered what she would carry in the crook of her arm,
what winter-object she would escort into the room and place
on the kitchen table as an offering of forgiveness, for in the flush
of their second winter together, he was never quite sure if she would
return in the morning for another chance at art.

"Paint me human today," she had said after yesterday's first fall
of virgin snow.
They had clung side by side at the window and fed the pigeons
bread, fogs of breath pouring from their lips as they stood so close
to the biting cold.
The magnificence of his own fantasy, a country scene, a vast
snow-white untouched by greed.
Each ripple of her breath, each bite of bread,

each cloud of steam from their mouths,
a crown of jewels he was certain
to embed in the afternoon paint.

But now it was morning and the long haul of the day lay before him.
He waited for her arrival with the same trepidation he had waited
for women through the years.
His women fled and returned, their hands carrying new hues,
new riches and spices and spoils from undiscovered places
he was frightened to travel to, for he was bound to a room.
The grandfather clock struck ten, and the swollen wind died down,
as if swallowing itself to nothingness.

Her beet-red lips moved, and he stepped back. He bent to his knees
and picked up the black cloth and flung it back over the canvas.
More sleep. They were all in need of more sleep.
Louis walked to the window and saw Patrice turn the corner,
a black hood over her head, a domino in the snow, a pink box
in the crook of her arm, a pink cardboard box filled with sugary-sweet.
He salivated with hunger and a well of relief settled him
as he reached out, touched the windowsill to hold himself up
for he was falling, falling in love with her quiet, with her secrets.

11. *Spring 1941*

MORE THAN ANYTHING IN THE WORLD, MORE THAN LIFE ITSELF, MORE THAN LOVE
AND SEX, MORE THAN MONEY AND FOOD, LOUIS LONGED FOR HIS PAINTINGS TO
HANG IN THE MUSEUM—HIS ART ENSHRINED IN THE WEALTHY TOMBS OF ART—THE
MASTERS' PAINTINGS ALL AROUND HIM. THE RESPECT THAT WAS THEIRS WOULD
BE HIS. IN THE SPRING OF NINETEEN HUNDRED FORTY-ONE, HADRIAN MET WITH
THE CURATOR. HADRIAN TOLD LOUIS: THE CURATOR WANTS MORE REALISTIC
PAINTINGS. ART IS ONLY A BUSINESS TO HIM. HE THINKS ARTISTS ARE PRIMA
DONNAS. HE THINKS ARTISTS SQUANDER LOVE. YOU ARE ONLY IMPORTANT TO
HIM AFTER YOU DIE. STILL, EVEN AFTER THE CURATOR'S REJECTION, LOUIS WAS
A BELIEVER IN MIXED SPECIES, IN OIL AND WATER, IN HORSES AND DONKEYS, IN
BANKERS AND PROSTITUTES, IN CURATORS AND VETERANS OF LOST WARS.

He surprised himself with the memory of another's painting. The economy
of the field. The minute details of specked earth, pebbled dirt and sand,
shooting blades of grass, a slight wind. A white house with a sloped thatched
roof in the horrible horizon. Window curtains drawn. A man beside a rock
waiting for the woman inside the house to open the window. It surprised him.
The memory of the outdoors painting.

He painted two black marks on the hardwood floor and positioned the two
legs of his easel firmly on the two black marks. He spread his paintbrush
like a rake and stepped into it, his favored left foot first.
Still, even after Hadrian shared the curator's rejection, Louis thought
the painter can, must, will threaded tugs and braided resistances,
oil-paintings, the mixing of species, the bland blended bond of pigment
to bone. White bone.
White stretched linen.
Still, even after the curator's rejection, Louis remembered the thrill of
staying inside the museum for hours, the museum guard watching him
with suspicious eyes,
the man's distrustful eyes on his skin as he roamed through the field
and smelled the Old Masters' land.

He remembered the French painter had his paints ground and delivered
to him wrapped in airtight pig bladders. "To paint smell is my goal,"
Louis said.
His unused hand grabbed the paintbrush with urgency of repetition,
for without it he would never create.

Laundered images rose to his mind as he dirtied the canvas grappled
with wild gestures of crucifixion. Crosshatches of black from north
to south from east to west. Repetitive motions soothed him and kept
him in a constant state of practice, gave him sustenance.
Brilliance and expression of feelings were born at the oddest
and unexpected moments when he remembered a dead painter.

He was tired. He yawned and moaned at his choices, wrestled
with Patrice's eyes watching him as he stole another artist's soul.
Bored with his life, with his existence, bored with the prescribed rising
and setting of the sun, he lit another cigarette and blew smoke
in her direction and flicked ashes to the hardwood floor.

"So it is with art, given to other artists, like an archaeologist who leaves
a piece unburied for the next hungry person that comes along," Patrice said.

He straightened his spine and painted her ears,
a tunnel of sepia-colored consumption.
A flood of words.
He carved a parable in her canal,
a story about a young boy walking alone in a furtive field.
He charted her body in longitudinal and latitudinal forms.
He created a map and renamed all her parts;
her right breast hung like a monk in perpetual prayer.

"Imagine how many times Virginia Woolf sat in her chair with cigarette
to lips and fought the urge not to burn her words," she said. "Imagine a
woman plagued by the canon of men. Imagine being the steward of earth
and unable to own land. Imagine an emancipated woman following in the
footsteps of men."

At the sound of her words he abandoned his map and charts and indulged
himself in a massive dig. His paintbrush shoved into a tube and emerged
in the air with a streak of phosphorescent-yellow and he dug and dug
the canvas with the love an archaeologist who kept one bone untouched
so the next man who came along would enjoy his fill too.

The paintbrush, a stick, a rod, a cane, the fire in his bones burned
a yellow field. The horizon melted with reaped dirt. Trees as human
figure sticks shot out from the earth. An armature of bones.

He painted the color of her hair, brown strands, woven and braided sex,
the leashed closed opening she kept to herself. No longer tired and short
of breath, he cobbled the ground with droppings of morning dew
on early-morning green Viennese grass.

All the while Patrice lay on the red velvet couch hungry for the world
of books and fairy tales. It was the spring condition she was in, her soul
far away, thousands of miles away shipwrecked and beached
on ancient rocks listening to the madness and cruelty of the sea.
"We are born in the same way, but express ourselves and die
in different ways," she whispered.

Awakened from a vision, as painful as being born,
he caught a glimpse of her very sadcolored face.

He brought back color to her cheeks as if stoking a fire back to life.
His brush breathed a vapor of green-white light on her flesh,
the hairs of his bristles, a near poet in the mist. He angled his brush
down. Slim-threaded shapely veins spread, nourished by history
that stretched back as far as five hundred years ago and beyond.

His breath pressed for more air as the silver band cinched to the paintbrush's
wood handle reflected like a mirror his dark Viennese eyes—a cherished time
when he stood in the field by the birch trees and saw from the window
his mother's face and winged arms calling him home for dinner.

"There are ten," Patrice said. "Ten themes in the world. Done and mastered
and recalibrated in different times. And yet, the notion of the modern tries
so desperately to erase the past."
"Name them," Louis said.
"Stranger comes into town. Birth. Life. Death. Redemption. War.
Love. Time. Sacrifice. And mystery."

12. Summer 1941

THE SOUNDS OF THE CITY SHUT HER DOORS, HER ENGINES, HER MACHINES,
BECKONED HER BABIES HOME. THE STREET VENDOR PACKED HER WARES AND
THE PROSTITUTE AMBLED TO HER CORNER AND THE MUSEUM GUARDS CHANGED
SHIFTS AND THE BAKER LAY HIS HEAD ON THE PILLOW AND THE ACTOR APPLIED
MAKEUP TO HIS CRUMBLED CLAY FACE AND MAGELLAN THE CHAUFFEUR DROVE
GABRIELLE CAMILLE GOTSALL THE RICH, UNHAPPILY MARRIED PATRONESS OF ART
TO HER HOME AND HADRIAN STOOD AT THE MAHOGANY BAR AND COUNTED HIS
TIPS AND MRS. ITO COVERED HER DYING PATIENT'S BODY WITH A WHITE SHEET
AND CLOSED HIS EYES.

They played with each other, bare barters of survival, pleasures
of the all-too-present moment—either, or—if you will, I will—love me more.
In the late afternoon hour, while the sun from the window stole
red hues as a vampire sucking blood, they danced this transaction
along the hardwood floor—his arm on her neck, her arm on the small
of his back—small, slip, slide steps and swoon sweeps across the hardwood
floor past the stationary grandfather clock, their bodies not touching
but breathing the imagination of sleepy-hollowed fantasy.

Patrice sank into the red velvet and she dug for the word, her metaphor
hidden in the crack underneath the pillow. As usual, she strung her words
with fine needle and thread, each letter a pearl, each line of her T a cross
between reality and fiction. Her hands barreled into the opening,
and she fondled the word with her fingers as if dipping her hardness
into the softness of powder, a pure-white floury sand. In the Cancerian air
she was certain of truth. Her truth, which lay hidden and hard as he tried
to penetrate her core, she, too, masked free verse. Her form. Her constraints
a Shakespearian sonnet, a haiku, the tightening of the rope, the loathing
and the despair and the hurt of humanity, for kindness no longer existed
in the bare barters of survival between them, no longer existed among
the terrible world outside, for they were a couple of fallen dreams,
for they all were deserted and fallen.

She guttered her summer thoughts and she roused her being in smell,
in his turpentine-infested world shapened, stretched, expansive,
and full of limitations. The scent of strawberries from the kitchen table
moved her to feel once again her reason for being and she opened
her mouth and he begged her not to move, the beginning of the dance,

his entry in, his opening to force his paintbrush into the membrane
of her brain, that tender spot of purple and blue capillaries, a complex
conclave of secretiveness.
She was curious why he was compelled to rein in her brain when
her breasts and her hands offered him the most pleasure a man
could endure. She pushed him to the south, her palm flat on his waist
turned him from the painting. She moved him backward in time and
Phoenician purple turned to scarlet-fever red.

"My lovely bones," she whispered into his ear. "Leave my brain alone,
paint my bones."

She lured him. She contained him. She gave him the image,
the one she held back hundreds of years before. She tortured him
with her anatomy, and his body weakened in her hold.
His dirty room turned clean, that moment when the bare barters of
survival tempted them with the truth, their primal love of the paints.

Her veins swelled with the fluidity of the moment and the painting
of her on the three-legged easel transformed, her lips parted as the
pigments like worms gnawed color killing color, scarlet-fever red
slaying Phoenician purple in the glorious warring month of June.
"There are no casual choices in art," she said. "You must choose."

13. FALL 1941

THE MOMENTARY HAPPINESS THAT HAD SURPRISINGLY FLARED INSIDE OF HIM
DIED AT THE SIGHT OF HER TURNING THE CORNER. HE RELUCTANTLY PULLED
HIMSELF FROM THE WINDOW. ALL OF A SUDDEN THERE SEEMED NOWHERE TO GO.
HE TORE THE BLACK CLOTH FROM THE CANVAS. THE PAINTING HAD BECOME
DISTASTEFUL AND WEARISOME. HE LOOSENED HIS SHIRT. HIS LIFE WAS A LIE.
YESTERDAY'S PAINTS HAD CHANGED DURING THE NIGHT. HIS LIFE WAS A LIE. AN
AIR OF ABANDONING A LIFETIME OF HABIT CARESSED HIS SKIN. THE AUTUMN
MORNING OUTSIDE HIS WINDOW SCREAMED AT HIM. HIS RIB CAGE FILLED
WITH SHALLOW BREATH. THE ILLUSION OF TIME SPREAD OUT FLAT ACROSS
THE CANVAS. HER PORTRAIT HAD GROWN EVEN MORE DEATHLESS DURING THE
NIGHT. SHE ENTERED THE ROOM CARRYING A RED LEAF. SHE PLACED IT ON
THE KITCHEN TABLE. HE BUSIED HIMSELF IN THE CORNER. HE MIXED THE PAINTS
WITH THE HANDS OF A MAN AS IF IT WERE TO BE HIS LAST TIME. SHE HAD
CARRIED THE WHOLE OF THE CITY INTO THE ROOM. THE RED LEAF SHONE ON
THE KITCHEN TABLE. ITS EDGES SHARP AS A KNIFE SHOUTED A DEEP LOVELINESS.
THE AUTUMN MONTHS HAD BECOME THEIR TIME OF YEAR WHEN THE EARTH
BETWEEN THEM PRIED OPEN AND LOUIS'S EYES FILLED WITH SORROWFUL
PRECIPITATION, AND PATRICE FORESHADOWED HIS MOROSE MOOD WITH THE
POSSIBILITY OF HOPE.

After she undressed, she was torn by the tenderness with which he wrapped
the blue terrycloth robe around her shoulders. It was as if she had awakened
from a centuries-old dream.

His hands radiated warmth and desire, although his fingers
did not touch her flesh. He stood behind her like a stone tower.
He breathed trust on the nape of her neck.
"You look ravishing in my robe."

If she chose to lean on him, if she let her body fall, he would be there
standing to catch her the way others had not caught her before.
Almost from the beginning she had found herself followed,
kept, watched, supervised. She lay on the couch, her front exposed,
her back pressed to the red velvet and yet she felt him in the rear,
following and watching, a shadow of artistry seducing her solitude,
both ensnaring and protecting her fear.
Standing on his feet all day, smoking cigarette after cigarette, he said,
"I warned you about painters. We cannot love."

She tiptoed to the couch. As she settled in the red velvet, his haunting
blue terrycloth robe draped over her knees. The tassel tied and tufted
at her waist, warmed her body like a painting of the man himself.
Patrice smelled the lasting impression in the robe, floundered blue,
a drowned and drawing stench of white sticky fluids embedded
in the threads. She felt warm and safe in his fireproof walls.
If there were a fire, if another homosexual like him forgot to extinguish
his cigarette, if there were a fire in The Metropolitan his paintings
would survive. Only paintings by possessive demented men burn.

The young girl's laughter downstairs faded and died. He removed
the blue terrycloth robe from her body and hung it on the bathroom door.

The blue robe hanged like the man himself, fell to the floor.
He studied the puddle of creases. "We cannot love, for we lie
to preserve our skin."

She rose from the couch, left a piece of herself on the couch.
"Fear," she said. "The one emotion most humans dream of.
You must learn to let go of nightmarish love." She bent to the floor and
covered herself with the robe. Her forefinger pushed into the pocket.
Tobacco curls. A book of matches. A teeth-marked pencil.
She fondled the blue robe, a pattern of intersections,
the mapped theology of it all, the bodily shawl.

The cloth of the blue terrycloth robe sent shivers down her spine.
She walked to the corner. She stood before him, with her back
toward him. They looked at her portrait for the first time together,
and she saw her image washed away like a candle-flame.
Her color gone. White cleaved to blue, blue consumed white.
Her shoulder bones flattened and soft.
Her suicidal heart, pierced with an arrow,
buried in layers of red-leaf trust.
Trust for the living and trust for the dead.

His chest and thighs pressed her back. Time became space.
They looked at the painting together with ravenous eyes
and a multitude of lies—they both heard terrible cries.
Impoverished, she grabbed his wrist and carried his hand
between her legs. "Beauty is far more enticing than truth," she said.

14. WINTER 1941

THE START OF DECEMBER BROUGHT WIND AND RAIN TO NEW YORK CITY. IN THE EARLY MORNING ON DECEMBER SEVEN, NINETEEN HUNDRED FORTY-ONE, PATRICE AND LOUIS WERE APART WHEN THE BOMBS DROPPED ON PEARL HARBOR TORCHING IT ALL AFLAME. MRS. ITO GREETED PATRICE AT THE TOP OF THE STAIRS. SHE CLUTCHED THE NEWSPAPER IN HER HAND. SHE TOLD PATRICE: MR. ITO IS DEAD. I FEEL IT IN MY BONES. THE BOYS HE GREW UP WITH KILLED HIM.

Louis took a cube of sugar and nibbled it. The glass jar of clean turpentine
on the three-legged table reminded him of a genius's brain. Lucid and calm
and contained, rank with minerals and poisons mined from earth.
The white powder dissolved in his mouth, flickered and fluent,
a fading coal along his tongue.
Sweet decadence. Special sustenance. Opiate. A religious moment.
Light-of-love white. He thought geniuses die poor—van Gogh sold
only one of his paintings while he lived. He laughed inside, and his abdominal,
pectoral, and dorsal muscles loosened underneath his winter wet clothes.
When the geniuses behind the bombs die, they too will die poor.

He uncovered the canvas, dropped the black cloth to the floor.
Behind him, steam engines sounded in the distant river all men ride.
Ahead of him in the morning darkness lay apologetic sadness.
The Lost Girl I Left Behind, finished and perched on the easel.
The inconstant woman. Her belly, raked filaments of bristle hairs
glistening and mimicking a sea of blue.

Patrice was late. Human beings were killing each other, and she was late.
Would she forgive him? Would she laugh at the name of the painting?
The Lost Girl I Left Behind, the sound of the seaside and the ever-taut white
sail of her dancing dress over her heirloom thighs. Her breasts confused him.
The cumbrous, rich-black soil he had raked the day before had sunk.
Her face now had the look of a terrible infant
and the drown of oceanic breath.

Yesterday she had asked him about his mother and had pilfered
his weaving and unweaving of himself with simple questions
as if she had two wings sewed to her chest and could soar to the sun
and her wings would not melt.

"Form of forms," she had said. "You can turn me into an animal
today if you wish. A winter lion's tale, the spiritual odyssey,
the reconciliation of a lost girl. Tell me the story of your mother today,
and I will lie silent on this cold tomb."

She was late, and he nibbled another sugar cube and held the minute
pieces of it between his own warrior teeth. Molten lava, the succulent
syrup in his mouth coated his throat and inside his chest.
Words were shallow and his feet wished for the commonplace world,
wished for the swallow of an ordinary man in an extraordinary place.
He nibbled a third sugar cube desirous of Earl Grey tea. She was late.
Outside they kill one another, and she was late. The painting was finished,
but he continued to pry at her flesh. *The Lost Girl I Left Behind* was finished,
and still he suffered unweaving and unraveling of his small self.
When she was late, when she trespassed time, she pulled his comic
and tragic past, steam-engines churned, and the fountain of nymphs
spilled and sprayed and the pigeons resided at his window dazed.

It was with a heavy heart she entered The Metropolitan carrying
brown-paper bags crossed at her chest. "The press of human
beings," she said, unpacking bags of sustenance and fragrances
to soften Pearl Harbor's catastrophic stench.

During the darkest hours of the year, Patrice tunneled her body
underneath the blue terrycloth, burrowed her hair and her face
away from eyes of passions and incisions of throats, closed her eyes
to heave her ship into the far, to a place where she stored her well of tears,
a cavern of violence witnessed in the darkest hours with the Italian artist
who painted her as a blue angel in the chapel of confession, the sweet
violet of afterlife.

During the darkest hours of the year, she covered her head with the blue
terrycloth robe and hid underneath the cloth eating and swallowing
one last, one lonely last winter pear.

She peered from under the cowl. "Paint me the color of violet,"
she whispered, "paint the missing lies of our unbearable winter truth."

She looked at the women on the walls. Bronze and gold eyes
watched her every move. She sensed their content days at home,
framed and hung by night, framed and hung by day to interior sane,
safe walls.
She sniffed her hand and placed it across the back of her neck.
In the darkest hours of the year, human beings were killing one another,
desirous of blood, while the women on the walls were fairer than most,
they became all, the choicest of all, tragic creatures stolen and sworn
in the spectrum of heavy hues, the artist's bodily sweat, swimming
in a pool of dark blue, the violent violet left side of his tremulous art,
the syncopation of his paint, winter truth, winter despair, long,
long winter days.
During the darkest and longest hours of the year, she lay low to the earth
while the women on the walls soared and watched the painter's hand,
a spent pawn of feathered love, quivering a hurried halo of violet breath.

And so he began a new painting, a woman hidden under a violet garbed hood,
holding on top of her palm a voluptuous pear, for hardly it mattered anymore
whether he posed her visible or concealed, for now he came to restore
her treasure-chest of linens and lamentations in all that she touched and held
as she hid her flesh from him, as she cursed the hands of time, as she fell
in love with the women hanging on his walls, a harem of sinful sirens
once crushed with stone, knowing, soaring and watching from afar
as the painter inched forward and attempted to reach out up close, as
the painter stepped backward and painted her body parts in reverse.

In the late afternoon, she was like iron, the hinge of her jaw rigid.
The biting cold seeped through the windowpanes and ran up and down
his spine. Despite the smell of turpentine, the smell of skinned pear
could not be stopped. Patrice lay held to herself, a secret lair of unmoving
diminutiveness, her playfulness stripped from her flesh, the shape of a
woman's face as smooth as the forged elements of iron.
The balance of nature gone. The terror and the sheer ecstasy diminished
by December's onslaught of cold.

Strange and cruel and romantic, she contained herself in winter's swallow.
A freedom in her stature grew more distant with the falling

coldness of snow. Even the plasma in her veins grew still.

He was tired of the terrible scenes he inflicted when he desired her
to unflinch herself, to give him a piece she secreted in her lair.
She knew the meaning of the world and refused him like a keeper
of the balance.
Still the air was cold, still he suffered, still she tortured him with her
serene look of content as he struggled with the daunting demons
he etched with ebony-black in the southernmost corner of the canvas.

He could almost hear the snow falling against the glass, crystals
crashing and atoms exploding and spreading down the smooth veneer.
He, too, held himself in a posture of forced contentment as she
reminded him during the darkest hours after the bombs dropped
on Pearl Harbor, "You are the one man living in the daring city
of the Americas, doing what he loves."

Still love, what did it matter in the face of her hidden secrets, in the lack
of entrance into her lair? If only she would invite him in, they could tea-party
themselves together in a fairy tale, but instead she ironed her way,
as if strength and an impenetrable stance empowered her with the truth.
Still the truth, he spread the ebony-black in a long gesture of contrast
dividing her body from the sky.
Still her rigidness, her iron would melt in spring and the memory
of chemical reactions he had applied in the black to increase its richness,
filled him with the conversation he desired from her lips.
Still it would come, still it was over when she broke her silence,
when her lips parted and she opened.

He turned from the canvas and peered at the fountain of nymphs,
a mound of now virgin snow, and he placed his paintbrush down and
walked to the red velvet couch. He handed her a loaf of braided bread,
and she held it in her hands, raised it to her mouth and tore the whole
in two parts. She leveled them on her palms, a scale of freedom on the left
and justice on the right, and in an angel's breath she whispered,
"Now, you must paint me the color of tears, the purest and whitest
sorrows we both sense outside."

He stepped back from the couch. Still the balance of nature
between them sent another wave of terror through his spine

as he walked back to the canvas and lifted his paintbrush in
his left, strongest and most frightened hand.
The abandonment of black plagued him with an absurd joy
he had not experienced in years. How natural it was to paint white
on a snowy December day, how surprisingly natural it was to paint
after the bombs dropped.

Wings. He gave her December's snow-white wings, angel wings in clouds
of distending harmony, for it was true, with each hour together they were
dying in December's mourned mouth, that time in history when the stopping
hard of devastation murdered their dreams, and took Mr. Ito, a poet,
from this world.

15. Spring 1942

EVEN IN SPRING, AFTER THE BOMBS DROPPED ON PEARL HARBOR, DAY AND NIGHT GROANED AND MOANED, BROODING OVER THE COUNTLESS DEATHS IN THE MORTAL WORLD. DAY AND NIGHT, THE WAR ON AMERICAN SOIL DESTROYED EVERY POSSIBLE COMFORT AND CAST A GLOOM ON THE FUTURE AS MEN PLOTTED REVENGE. MRS. ITO CONTINUED TO WORK AT THE HOSPITAL. MRS. ITO GREETED PATRICE ON THE STAIRS. THE NEWSPAPERS HAD REPORTED EVACUATION. JAPANESE AMERICANS WERE BEING INTERNED IN CAMPS. MRS. ITO EXPRESSED HER FEAR THAT AN EVER-GROWING FUROR OF HATRED FOR THE JAPANESE WOULD RESULT IN SOMETHING TERRIBLE, SOMETHING SO HORRIFIC WAS TO PASS OVER AND DECIMATE THE LAND OF THE RISING SUN.

The sky showed Louis a pattern, truth after truth thrown on one another,
one obliterating the other, the tender air of hurt and banishment, a devil
hand lurking in the firmament, a fist so eager to take away. He piled
and suffocated meanings to discover something Patrice hid from him,
the edge of a crevice she harbored in the palm of her hand, the crescent
smile she coveted in the corner of her lip. His room was like an oven.
His generous arms flung like wings to guard off the heavy black sky
outside his window. An heir to reality, with each new abstraction,
he abandoned tinges of bright color. A wide wingful brushstroke of black
and purple masked matter, diffused definition, fused texture, fanned
titillating chaos across the landscape of Patrice's springtime flesh,
her secreted April realm.

Specimens of pleasure forfeited as he smuggled implements
of her sorrow through gates, as his white-sleeve arm wavered
and hung like a warred piece of white cloth pinned to a taut
clothesline blowing surrender in the wind.

His eyes telescoped the sky's rich black. He lashed cracks,
fractured spider-black, a withered web of his mother's darkest
heart, the one bedded in Franz's art. He heard his mother's cry,
he knew her last sound, he divined her desire to live and endure.
He prepared his ritual of laying out his paints in a circle around
himself on the floor. Tinges of color, particles of the physical world,
cooled the heat, soaked his burning sensation. He felt the weight
of his liver. He planted his own meaning into his vaulted cell,
forever inquisitive and never wholly understandable.

"Don't paint my anatomy today. Paint me different. I hide nothing
from you today. I hid everything from you yesterday," Patrice said,
pressing her lips into the red velvet crack where she hoarded
her most intimate truths.

*He plucked a handful of lilies from the floor, and he laid the stems
at her feet, a mound of pillowed purple at the bottom of the painting.
They had called his mother a whore. He heard the invisible whisper
of the Viennese crowd, the ones damaged from love. For years he had
painted his mother as purple dust, the ash of conceived lustful passion.
For years she was his purple field. He daubed her lilies-of-the-valley trail,
sprinkled the salt of the roiling washing ocean wave after wave along
her endangered shore.*

The sky showed him the resilience of the afterlife.
His mother's cloaked return.
He awaited her arrival, felt her coming, his mother's tender footsteps
marching to his side, to touch his wings, to rearrange his pattern,
to depossess his lack of faith.
His stomach, kidney, and liver ached as her ashen face embalmed
his entrails with names, sacred names of lovers who dare not speak
its name, her mouth and her teeth unable to press the wind-wheel of change
between the folds of her lips as she ferried herself across alone.
The sky showed him the pattern of portrait, that elusive state of pressing
his body into the skinned beauty of Patrice's sacrum, for he was tired
of painting her eyes and her nose and her mouth.

*He inched through the entry, his breath heavy with guilt.
The passage through the rear was dark and coated with sadness,
sorrow dripped from cavern walls, a cistern echoed.
His bristles as a broom traversed the mounds of her buttocks,
a desert of drifted, hot, sweltered sand, an hourglass of sand seeping
and slipping and sounding the promise of dawn.*

Patrice's toes stretched over the edge, clambering for the lion's paw.
She was the mistress of her field.
She slowly caressed the chestnut lion's paw with her warm toes.
Her index finger rose to her mouth, before she spoke, silencing
the forbidden, mourning the loss, censoring the innocence, swallowing
the hurt feelings in her black fragile vaulted cell throat.

"I am not afraid," she said. "He takes from you, but he gives me more and more." She lifted her elbow in the air, a tiller of bone.

The sky showed him the tender spot. The one untouched arena, unearthed, unstained. Her grandeur in all that had been pilfered, stolen, and sold, the reality of hurt scribed in the canopy overhead.

He painted a shaft of light, a lighthouse white beam saving the scrutiny
of the sea, her hidden treasures, swells of currents from the bowels
of her abdomen as she stretched a limb, as her thigh sighed and
her heel descended and her toes curled and heaved to the lion's paw
for a moment of reprieve.

His mother appeared. Her arms like sparrow wings intercoursed shadows across her flesh. "I have come all this way to tell you . . . you are not ready to receive."

He did not recognize her voice. Her voice sounded different from Louis's memory of his mother. Her voice was not the voice in his imagination that had lived on.

He was thrust from Patrice's field. He was pushed out and away and drowned farther in her black and purple toes like his father's hand on his back, throwing him to the floor, like the color of Louis's boyfriend who one day disappeared into his father's library and never returned—one truth after truth thrown down on one another, one obliterating the other in the family vaulted hell.
He sucked in air, and his mother disappeared.

16. Summer 1942

LOUIS LOOKED AT THE GRANDFATHER CLOCK, TALL, TOWERING, GALLANT AS A MAN
IN A CORNER WITH HIS FACE TO THE WALL CONTEMPLATING HIS BEGINNINGS, HIS
ENDINGS. A MAN SO TERRIBLE, SO ALONE. PERHAPS ALL ALONG LOUIS HAD BEEN
PAINTING THE WRONG THING—HE HAD BEEN PAINTING HER, BUT REALLY IT WAS
HIS OWN SELF-PORTRAIT HE PAINTED UNDERNEATH HER SKIN.

She was stretched on her elbows as if she were embryonic about to give birth
to a great ideal. She was stretched as if she were delivering a message that
he must decode. He rubbed the corner of the painting with his thumb and
memorized her pose. With small circle-swipes he gravitated to the center,
and her repose, her flesh under control of the spirit implanted itself in his
August mind. For it was the last month of the summer and he was intent on
reaching completion, he was intent on removing layers of skin and muscles
and bodily fluids to understand the nature of the woman more.

He began with her profile, a line from her brain that veered alongside
his reserved breath. He shaped her forehead, her nose, her eyes, her lips,
and her chin. The positive magnification of the material parts of a face,
the hierarchy from the posterior wall of the head, a downward pull
to the water well, the mouth.

A single ruling passion, the melancholy of her smile, the smooth alabaster
veneer of her skin, and the embedded secrets she kept to herself,
unbounded the terrible silence between them in the late morning hours
when she settled deeply in the velvet as if she were falling into soft red grass.
"Tragedy and comedy come from the same letters," she said through her
faint smile.

He doctored himself. He lit a cigarette and
he orchestrated his next movement,
his memory of her stretching now lost over time
as her time stole his most delicious moments.
He nourished himself. He kept his eyes affixed to her neck.
He held his paintbrush in his right hand, his cigarette between his lips,
and with his thumb he rubbed fingerprints into her neck.

He fed the color of Naples yellow with texture. He released his subject,
ridges spread like canyon walls, the erosion of earth's solid armature.

The choreography of desire at the moment of surrender filled him
with courage. He removed the cigarette from his lips and placed it
in the ashtray. Smoke furled across his canvas and shadowed his
submission to her embryonic air.

She lifted her arm and the shape of her elbow disappeared. She opened
her eyes, and he felt her penetration. He nursed himself with her fondness
of hope. It was August and surely he deserved more words she refused to
share. He waited with patience, his thumb pressing Naples yellow's radiant
strength in the darkest crevices of her neck.

He would paint her one hundred times, a thousand times until there
was no longer anything left to understand, until he had figured her out.
He would stay with Patrice year after year until there was no longer
any dangling mystery to solve. He would stay with her in the same way
a writer rewrites the same theme over and over again until there is nothing
left to solve. Louis (a man of habit) would paint her day after day
until her body turned into something else. He would kill her and
resuscitate her, rework her, reinvent her so that her spirit remained.
He would paint fiction. Neither facts nor lies.

"Only the unauthentic is ugly in art. If you continue to deceive
yourself, then you deceive art," she said.

The illustrious innocence of her voice filled him with fear of the unknown.
She had disturbed his order, she had once again discovered his weakness.
He opened his palm, and he kneaded her neck as if he were sculpting
with pellets of clay.

She curled into a ball, stared at his black-leather, laced shoes, flat heels
and pointed toes that touched the hardwood floor like two sharp-flinted
arrows aiming at her lying on the red velvet couch.

BOOK TWO

FALL

17. FALL 1942

AUTUMN IN THE CITY EXISTED IN THE SAME MANNER AS BEFORE. HER CLOTHES SMELLED OF SPICES, OF MARCO POLO GOLD. PATRICE BROUGHT LOUIS MYRIAD FRAGRANCES SHE CARRIED INTO THE ROOM. SALT-OF-THE-EARTH SPICES, DUG FROM THE GROUND, CARTED AND HAULED TO THE CITY TO BE SOLD. WOMEN WHO GREETED MORNING SHIPS TO PURCHASE SCENTS. WOMEN IN NEED OF OTHER-THAN-DECAYING CITY SCENTS. LOUIS WONDERED WHERE HAD SHE BEEN? WHAT SHIP HAD SHE SAILED DURING THE EVENING? HOW MANY EXPLORERS' HANDS HAD TRAVELED ALONG HER SKIN?

He had only to open his eyes, to see the time, the flaked decibels
of melody that hung to the walls,
the diminutive sounds of their conversation,
their passions now hushed by the hourglass of time,
sand passing and pissing away,
her saliva immersed in the interior chamber of their time together,
savaged time, time-pilfered riches stolen from the outside world.

He had only to open his eyes, to see his own fear, his own slippage
and mistakes, the extremity of his moods, flattened to the plastered walls,
his rows of paintings gallantly preening his history.
The day he moved swift.
The day he crawled with the paws of a tiger in search of prey.

He lumbered out, moved from the corner and positioned himself
in the sun's rays.
The arrows pierced his chest and in a moment of completion,
he signed his fate to her with a bow of forgiveness.
Tired of the hurt and her desire to escape, Louis stood
between Patrice and the light and shaded her from the atmospheric spill,
the scattering of light and darkness forming a chord of shadows
throughout the room.

His eyes were drawn to the window.
The vanishing point, his perspective, that place where he began
so many miles away,
thousands of meters away to the east in the opera house of Vienna
where the red velvet chairs were stained with tragedy's love sweat,
the squandering of women and men in desperate need of the heart's core.

Patrice had asked him to paint from the new world, to find her hidden point
she kept for him in the fall, like a hibernation, a nation of stored riches
all women keep for men.

But he was intent, still intent on painting from his homeland,
the memories of the masters left in the crevice of time,
time when he was a boy and his mother
raised her white handkerchief to her face
wiping away the tears.

Salt, the substance of both fire and water, he had painted into yesterday's
paint, the brine from the bottom of the deep-blue sea that separated
him from Vienna, the membrane that kept him clean and preserved his
antiquities—the masters, those who did not listen to the criticism and
judgment of other men, those whose spirits he felt in the Viennese opera
house, when his mother, in her black dress raised the white handkerchief
like a bandage to her eyes and wiped away her tears, her sins.
But how was he to know of sin at such a young age?

And now, how was he to know if his mother had cried? How was he
to know if she had heard the violins? How was he to know if she had
detached herself from the human hands that played her dirgesong
when she walked past the Nazis to the gas chamber?

If he had only opened his eyes, the desire to be alone with himself would
diminish. If he were to open his eyes, he would see her hiding place,
for Patrice was void of deception and she, too, had loved, had sat
in the red velvet chairs and witnessed the divine tears falling, hesitating
and falling spellbound from the sorrowed eyes of women who came
to the hall to escape time.

He licked his tongue.
The salt tasted good.
The salt made him thirsty.
He wrestled with the salt, his tongue rubbing small pebbles along his lower
lip, and his perception of reality, a well of saliva in the cave of his mouth,
drowned him, drowned his morose morning mood as high noon turned
so magnificently into afternoon.

Patrice whispered, "Louis, I, too, hear, the, violins, we are not alone."

He stepped back to the canvas, and the light through his body darted in
her direction. She held up her arms and shielded her eyes from the sun's
rays as if it were too early in the day to saturate her entire being in light.

He dipped his paintbrush in autumn-orange, first in red, then in yellow,
and he circled a halo above her melancholic head in the northernmost
part of the canvas. An operatic garland.
A galaxy of glowing Viennese night stars.

18. WINTER 1942

AT LUNCH HE RAN HIS PALMS OVER THE WHITE CLEAN TABLECLOTH (HE KEPT A DRAWER FULL OF WHITE CLEAN TABLECLOTHS). HE SET THE TABLE AND OPENED A BOTTLE OF WINE. THEY ATE CHEESE AND BREAD AND FRUIT FROM ONE PLATE. THE DISTANCE BETWEEN THEM AT THE TABLE WAS THE SPACE BETWEEN A DEAD BODY AND THE LID OF A COFFIN, A PURE HOLLOW SPACE. THEY DID NOT TOUCH EACH OTHER. THEY DID NOT USE FORKS, KNIVES, OR SPOONS. FOR NAPKINS THEY LIFTED THE WHITE TABLECLOTH THAT HUNG ON THEIR LAPS AND WIPED THEIR MOUTHS. AFTER THEIR MEAL, IN LOUIS'S PAINTING, HER HANDS WOULD BE YOUNG AGAIN. THEY WOULD REACH A LONG WAY ACROSS THE WHITE TABLE ON THE CANVAS, ALMOST, BUT NOT GRASPING HADRIAN'S WINE BOTTLE THAT HAD FALLEN AND LEFT A BURGUNDY STAIN ALONG HIS WHITE EMPTY SPACE.

The shadow of his smile. It seemed to her as she sipped the red wine
that was almost the first thing she had felt about him. He was a creature
of habit with an impenetrable hold, but the crack in his lips came
at the most extraordinary moments
as if he were breathing air for the first time,
as if he would at any time,
never breathe air into his lungs.

The shadow of his smile lay underneath, and the corners of his canvas,
the spokes of his shadows, gave the private parts of himself away
to the eyes of those desperate for the imaginative parts of themselves
missing in the tracts of stolen time.

A stale air grew between them through the three and a half years
they were together, but the wine, a permanent fixed sense still warmed
her blood and flowed through her veins. That was almost the first thing
she had felt about him, his playful love of her colors, his appreciation
for the scents she carried in his room, the way he devoured her desserts
as a child eating after punishment.

But the shadow of his smile, the dark cushion of his mother's death,
his father's death, his grandfather's death, the deaths of Jews
the deaths of his homosexual friends, his insipid masculine desire
to master her body, not the art, kept her bound to the red velvet couch,
kept her funded in independence and brilliance as she led him
through the corridors of her thread.

A barrage of light splattered the wineglass, and the blood of grapes
turned to that magnificent shade of coral tongues, and she closed
her eyes and mired her feet into the sinking red sand. The stealing
hours of the shadow of his smile kept her in touch with her nature.
He wished to die, but she had to keep him alive until they reached
her desired end.

She sensed a note of menace in the sweep of his brush. "Listen to me,"
she said in a hoarse voice. "We have no self until we learn to keep our
secrets. In the felt of art, secrecy must be observed."

What happened, then happened, the going and coming moved swiftly,
the elliptical nature of the early afternoon sun twirled and swirled
with wild, and she lifted her chest toward the ceiling and her bones opened.
In the vein of giving, she gave him a slim piece of her heart, her ventricle
churned the redness of the wine, and the city outside his window turned
silent in illumination and she listened to his lungs gasping for breath,
groping for color, and he angled his paintbrush to the floor, the gravity
of earth pulled his shadow of a smile into a pasture of pure, he was inside,
he roamed and he swam, careful not to tear at her walls. For a long while
neither said a word nor breathed a thought.

He blew cigarette smoke her way, and the bottled winter smile
of his disenchantment that was the last gesture she remembered
as he spread her narrative with the deepest blues and the blackest black
and flowered her insides with the yellow sorrow of his past and with
the scripture he thought he needed in death.

19. *Spring 1943*

WHEN PATRICE ENTERED THE ROOM SHE BENT TO PICK UP THE CRUMPLED CHARCOAL SKETCHES OFF THE HARDWOOD FLOOR, AND SHE KEPT HER KNEES TOGETHER EXTENDED IN THE OPPOSITE DIRECTION TO BALANCE HER BODY. SHE UNDRESSED AND LAY ON THE RED VELVET COUCH AND TOLD HIM: YOU CANNOT JUST DISCARD SOMETHING THAT YOU NO LONGER LOVE. THE MALADOUS, MALICIOUS MORNING SUN POURED THROUGH THE WINDOWS. THE PURPLE TULIPS MRS. ITO BROUGHT HIM YESTERDAY REMAINED RUBBER-BANDED, STILL WRAPPED IN PLASTIC, PETALS TIGHTLY CLOSED. THE CLOCK CHIMED NINE TIMES. PATRICE WAS AFRAID TO LOOK AT THE GRANDFATHER CLOCK BECAUSE SHE HAD PROMISED HERSELF NOT TO ALIGN HERSELF WITH TIME. WHEN LOUIS ASKED: WHERE ARE YOU FROM?, SHE LOWERED HER CHIN, LIFTED HER EYEBROWS, DROPPED THE CORNERS OF HER MOUTH, RAN HER TONGUE ALONG THE TENDER FOLD OF HER UPPER LIP AND ANSWERED: THE DEAD SEA. EACH DAY SHE ANSWERED HIS INQUIRY ABOUT HER ORIGIN WITH SOME PLACE NEW.

Today she wore the scent of his mother, a rare kind of butterfly,
the maladies of her soul, thick, honeyed wings of despair.

She fingered the shawl around her shoulders, ran her hands
through the primitive black and yellow threads, like a monarch
bedecked on a throne, each touch a note of affirmation, identity,
sanity, an exhausted state of love.

Afar in the distance she fluttered her eyelids as he grafted her butterfly skin
with the cool metal edge of the palette knife, peeled her outmost to unearth
the birth of her pollinated smell.

She wrapped the shawl around her neck and combed the tassels
with her fingers as if she combed the hair of her child, that lonely girl
on a bed of sand, the smell of a rare butterfly near to the sea.

She heard the tenderness of the young girl's freedom, a moment
of excitement she swallowed in her spring throat.

"I remember," she confessed, "coal burning in the fireplace, the walls
of his house, a black coffin, the inside of his soul a white dove, his pose,
his passion, his purse, his resistance, his candlelight shadows dancing on
his dirty walls. I remember how he ate the livers and hearts of cows

and spewed me garbed in red velvet and lace, my head a virgin, my hands
a garland of thorns, my feet perched on a white clean pillow, clouds
overhead, pastoral paradise, my bucolic body cloaked in red velvet wine,
neither portrait nor beautiful, the sadness of my face, tears welled down
my cheeks. I remember he painted me among his waterwave of hate,
disdain for my riches, my youth, my ability to peer in his heart and suck
his good, how he wanted to be bad, to live among the dead painters,
your friends, the romantic romancing the hidden stone. And then I
remember the Inquisition, the paintings he hid of me, in his garden,
a hole he dug, the paintings of me piled in the ground, one on top of the
other, the carriage that drove me from his town, my innocence submerged
in the soul of worms, the sound of white and black horses galloping over
my tomb, his desire to preserve me among the ruins, my ruddy-red cheeks
embodied the dark damp earth as they dragged him from his studio,
chained his wrists to wood and burned him." She stopped for breath.

"Louis, you are not alone. We all come from a history
of catastrophic desertion."

20. Summer 1943

THE MORNING CITY BEFORE HIM RECEIVED NO ILLUMINATION FROM THE SKY
OR THE BROOKLYN BRIDGE OR THE EAST RIVER. WHEN PATRICE ENTERED THE
ROOM SHE BECAME THE COLOR OF THE ROOM, HER SKIN LIKE A MIRROR, A
PRISM. SHE BECAME EVERY COLOR. SHE WAS JADE GREEN AND GRANITE CLAY
RED. SHE UNDRESSED AND LAY ON THE COUCH LIKE A PRESSED FLOWER ON
A PAGE. THE PORTRAIT OF PATRICE RESIDED ON THE EASEL FULL OF PROMISE
AND RIDDLED WITH A SPELL OF INCOMPLETENESS. LOUIS BROODED OVER THE
SURFACE STEADFASTLY LOOKING FOR A FLAW. EARLIER HADRIAN AND MRS.
ITO HAD TOLD HIM HE HAD CAPTURED AN ESSENCE THAT HAD NEVER EXISTED
BEFORE, BUT HE COULD NOT LOOK AT THE PAINTING WITHOUT SEEING FAULT,
SOMETHING HE LEFT OUT, SOMETHING THAT CRIED OUT FOR MORE.

It was the best hour of the day. Patrice's skin was moist and content.
The afternoon dampness settled in the velvet like wet sand, the shedding
of her perfume lingered in the space between them, resurrected
blossomed orchids erect in a glass vase. A turn-of-the-century noise hummed
in the background. Patrice's weariness was gone, the spin, twirl, and madness
lessened as she sailed to a new horizon of heightened existence.

It seemed as though the whole of the room was mourning
summer's near-end. The last color of summer stuck to his bristles,
and the sweep of a strong and more powerful heir to summer's throne
made him intoxicated as each useless hour drained breath out of him.
He felt orphaned. He felt accidental. He felt abandoned and useless
as she crept farther and farther away from him. He contemplated
the choicest color of all amid this pure agony of mortal time.
Motherless and fatherless, he stood before the painting at a loss,
powerless, crossing a vast unknown.

He blurred the outlines of her flesh. The precarious paintbrush spread
and stretched her veneer, while the afternoon simmered to an end and
warmed her to the hour, to the rare moment when the painter refrained
from destructive thoughts and formed a union with only his paints and
transplanted her into the ground like a rooted tree, a permanent attachment,
no longer a nomad but a woman with a land to claim as her own,
her own home, her own castle, her own captive tower.

There was a break in the clouds. Showered by afternoon's first shout

of the sun, rays darted into the room, pierced his back and sharp-shot
a slew of arrows in her direction. The damp and moist velvet dried up
like the skin of an aging woman.

When she had carried the pink cardboard box into the room and placed
it on the kitchen table, she had waited for this moment, for the best hour
of the day when he threw his paintbrush down and the swish of the bristles
heralded the stoppage of time, and together, she and he, woman and man,
sat at the table and fed each other sweets, her small hand spooning his
mouth with sugar, and his turpentine-infested fingers tearing the pastries
into morsels, dividing delicate mouthful parts like a man not interested in
the whole, only enamored with the infinite possibilities and the hierarchy
of objects, the loftier the better, the smaller the stronger, the sweeter the
memory of tart.

And so they were in the best hour of New York City, when the clock wound
down, when time moved slower and slower and the day reached the acumen
of being longer, each moment closer to his death, each moment his paints
growing with blossoming color, her perfumed orchids entrenching
its unbottled essence with the most magnificent fragrance, the kind
of smell Patrice needed to stay alive, the kind of hour she lived for
with each waking breath.

As hunger subsided and the sugar in their blood awakened their senses,
they kept their conversation a secret, they spoke to each other without
words, they swallowed and digested, and closed the pink cardboard box
and returned to their natural poses. He moved in the corner, his chest
huffed and puffed, consumed with the insane desire to create, long legs,
lewd legs, wandering legs, inferior legs, inferior paints.
She moved slowly on the red velvet couch, her body sprawled out
as the afternoon serenely left the room leaving them alone like two
strangers in desperate wait of night.

An hour passed. Louis lit a candle, and Patrice smelled almond burning,
wax dripping on wood, wax melting away. She closed her eyes.
The young girl downstairs pounded the ivory and onyx piano keys.
The young girl rushed to reach the end of the song, the passionate
classical score of a musician who had lived through wars.
Louis lay down beside Patrice and rested his head on her breasts
and cried as he had cried as a boy.

21. FALL 1943

PATRICE DID NOT CARRY AN UMBRELLA WHEN IT RAINED. SHE WALKED TO THE
METROPOLITAN, CLOSE TO THE CURB, DISTANCING HERSELF AN ARM'S LENGTH
FROM THOSE HURRYING BESIDE HER. THE CITY A CLOUD OF GREY, SHE GREETED
THE DOWNPOUR UNPERTURBED AND DESIROUS OF RAIN. SHE HEARD SWISHING
TAXI WHEELS, HISSING WINDSHIELD WIPERS, SPLASHING PUDDLES, MOURNFUL
PRECIPITATION. NO LOVE IN THE RAIN, ONLY SUFFERING ALONGSIDE THE RAIN,
THE WORLD MOVED UNAWARE OF THE TEARS THAT FELL ON ITS BEHALF AS THE
CROWD TRAVELED UNDERNEATH BLACK UMBRELLA DOMES, SAFE AND DRY, A
FUNERAL PROCESSION, THOUSANDS OF ANTS MARCHING TO WORK WEARING
BLACK HATS. AT THE ENTRANCE TO THE PARK, SHE STOOD SHELTERED UNDER
THE MARBLE ARCH. A MAN WORE A BLACK BERET, WRAPPED IN AN ARMY-GREEN
BLANKET, A TIN CAN AT HIS FEET. THREE GREY PIGEONS WITH PINK-AND-BLUE
WINGS PECKED AT THE MAN'S BROWN-PAPER BAG. PATRICE THREW SILVER COINS
IN HIS TIN CAN. THE BIRDS FLEW AWAY. PATRICE ARRIVED AT THE METROPOLITAN
DRENCHED. LOUIS HANDED HER A TOWEL. SHE SMELLED OF THE OUTDOORS.
HER ADOLESCENT SMILE HAD THE LOOK OF ENNUI, HER CHIN THE SHAPE OF
THE EDGE OF A NEW MOON. SHE WIPED HER FACE AND UNDRESSED AND THREW
HER CLOTHES IN A PILE ON THE HARDWOOD FLOOR. LOUIS PLACED HIS BLUE
TERRYCLOTH ROBE OVER HER SHOULDERS. HE SAID: YOU SMELL GOOD LIKE
THE INSIDE OF A LILY IN A FIELD AFTER RAIN. PATRICE LAY ON THE COUCH. SHE
ARCHED HER NECK AND SAID IN A GRAVELLY VOICE: TO SMELL LIKE THE INSIDE
OF A LILY AFTER RAIN. I WOULD LIKE TO BE REMEMBERED FOR THAT. PERHAPS
YOU CAN PAINT THAT TODAY.

The hours were more sumptuous than usual during autumn. The rainy
world outside his window looked more beautiful than ever before.
The failure of the paint diminished as the pigments settled into the surface
like water in the ground. The movement of his brushstrokes unattached,
his intention and his ego disappeared with each tired time-sweep of the
pendulum of the grandfather clock.
Pith of memory clung and the object he once loved was swallowed
in the teeth of a storm. Weather's blast of rain and cold, leaving
him poised to abandon and dwell.

She looked like a reptile resting on a red leaf. The illumination of rain poured
through the window and showered her ancient skin with beads of wet.
The truth of the city lay hidden underneath her clothes. Her promiscuous air
and her celebration and her luxuriousness came to him when she had disrobed

her transgressions and humiliation as she undressed, piling each garment
that oozed city waste, one on top of the other in a mound on the floor
as if she were shedding layers and layers of dead skin.

She rested her head on the pillow, a quiet thud, in his walls, the voice
of unlove. Her hands swarmed and traveled the valley of the velvet,
the vale of unlove. She caressed the throne where the women on the walls
once lay, where she now lay and others would lie, come to the painter and lie.

He trawled his hands through the air and glazed his paintbrush in desert-gold
and he sleared a brilliant plumage from the crown of her head and he embedded
tiny specks of flecked golden jewels in the irises of her eyes.

"Have you ever loved?" she asked in a soft whisper.
"Never," he said. The paintbrush fell from his hand.
Primitive desert-gold splattered his toes.
"What about Hadrian?"
"The world once was ready for us, but no longer is," he said in a grave voice.

She blushed and hid her hands safe underneath her thighs. In the shallows
of her throat she counted her fingers the way a mother examines her child.
She closed her eyes and fell into the forgotten grains of sleep, each moment
leaving him alone in the room to tend for himself.

He loosened his clothes, and he staggered in the corner. Desirous of
love, he sulked in his corner. A filament of darkness covered his eyes.
The painting smelled of Vienna and coal and the dark edge of his crushed
universe. He felt held captive like a kidnapped bird in a city cage.
He wished for more rain. He sucked on the tip of the paintbrush,
teeth-marks of weaponry biting the wood.

Franz had told him not so hard, not so hard, but he could not stop himself.
He waited for the light to come and cast its spell and free him from
the dark prison of his past.

He lifted the paintbrush from the hardwood floor. Unabashed desert-gold
still stuck to his sable bristles. He wiped his paintbrush on the turpentine-
soaked rag that hung from his waist and he dabbed his clean brush in a pool
of stagnant blue he had mixed earlier for this precise moment. He painted
a sailor-blue lavender face.

"When I die they will ask you questions," he said.

She opened her eyes and parted her lips and smiled the feminine mouth she gave to him when the end of pelting rain altered the sorrow and pity and the dread and the narcotic pain that swathed their existence.

"What kind of questions?" she asked in the naïve voice she saved for late afternoon.
"They will ask if we were lovers," he said.
"Lovers?" she repeated.
"Lovers," he said again, his paintbrush descending from her now radiant sapphire-blue eyes to her reptilian neck to the selvage of the red leaf.
"Let them translate your life as they wish, as it fits their needs. To be remembered as a man's lover is not what I have come all this way for."

22. WINTER 1943

PATRICE AND LOUIS SPENT THEIR DAYS TOGETHER AND THEIR NIGHTS APART
FROM EACH OTHER. PATRICE CARRIED A PIECE OF HIM HOME EVERY DAY. WHEN
SHE LEFT AT DUSK, HE HANDED HER A LOAF OF BREAD, AND SHE CARRIED
MORSELS OF HIM LIKE FLOUR AGAINST HER FLESH. IN THE PARALLEL STREETS
OF THE CITY THAT STRETCHED INTO INTERSECTIONS, PATRICE WAS ACCOSTED
BY LOCOMOTION, A MULTITUDE OF TRIALS AND TRIBULATIONS, RARE BREEDS
OF HOWLS, A WHIRLPOOL OF ADVENTURE, CROWNED JEWELS, AND NUMEROUS
UNBROKEN VOWS, CRIES FOR HELP, MOANS OF CONSUMMATED LOVE. MRS. ITO
RETURNED FROM THE HOSPITAL TO THE METROPOLITAN AFTER WORK. SHE
PERFORMED RITUALS TO PURIFY HER SOUL. SHE OPENED HER ALTAR, LIT INCENSE,
AND SAID A PRAYER TO HER BELOVED DEAD HUSBAND SHE HAD BEEN MARRIED
TO FOR THIRTY YEARS. SHE SPRINKLED SALT OVER HER HEAD TO RID HER BODY
OF SICKNESS AND DEATH THAT CLUNG TO HER SKIN. SHE ATE A BOWL OF WHITE
RICE AND STEAMED VEGETABLES. SHE WENT TO VISIT LOUIS AND HE SAT BESIDE
HER ON THE COUCH. SHE OPENED A BLACK VELVET SATCHEL AND INSERTED
SMALL STERILIZED ACUPUNCTURE NEEDLES IN PAINED AND BLOCKED POINTS
OF HIS BODY THAT SHE HAD LEARNED FROM HER TEACHER BEFORE SHE LEFT
JAPAN TO MARRY MR. ITO IN NEW YORK CITY AS WAS ARRANGED BY HER FAMILY.
ON SOME NIGHTS, AFTER THE WHITE RABBIT CAFÉ CLOSED, HADRIAN CAME TO
LOUIS TO FALL ASLEEP IN HIS ARMS.

In the cold black night Louis pressed himself to the window and smelled
the sea-damp. Palms flat against the glass, he listened to the empty ships,
wooden bowels anchored to the berth, the rough sound of steel rubbing
wood like a defeated body chained to its maker.
It hurt.
The cold cry of the night tortured, tied, demented, tired. In the distance,
waterwaves flapped, fins of river flesh pushed from the sea, and behind
him blood dripped from her vein down the landscape of his paint.

He rested his forehead between his hands, and his eyes surveyed
the magic, lights dimmed like a strung lantern from tree to tree.
The carnival dead, traveled on in the late-night early-morning gallows
of darkness.

She was missing. The moon a deceptive dancer,
hidden behind a tall building—
stripping her clothes and removing her pearls, alone.

A voice spoke out of the shadows at his side.
The tender voice of only one person he knew.
His mother now waited and came when Patrice, Mrs. Ito, and Hadrian left,
as if she were uninvited when others were around.
His mother came when he needed her most, shrill of a sparrow flying
around his paintings, eyes preening for jewels.
His mother begged for him to speak to her, to scold her, to punish her,
to remind her of the acts she had committed before him as a child.
The city welcomed her, shone her out of the vaulted cell
with a veil of lightness, robbed her of color and clothes.

His legs lessened when she was in the room.
He shrank in her presence and sank closer to the floor.
He kept his back to the painting and leaned his forehead and two hands
to the glass, in reverence.
Franz had told him never look upon art with anything less than devotion.

The greats, they, too, bowed to his mother whenever she entered the room.
They, too, sensed the plenty she harbored in her field, the small roundness
of her belly and the angles of her thighs and the shoot of her neck,
the madness and wildness of her rampaged brain.
Louis had inherited her hurt and swallowed her pride and hid her secrets
under layers of paint.

The buried came alive on cold black nights when he was hungry
for love, when his desire to step outside consumed and devoured
his impulse to paint.
The sea-damp and the empty, antique-cinched, tin tube of white
and the biting cold glass against his skin embalmed him,
kept him imprisoned to the view.

He licked his index finger and drew a circle around himself along
the glass, and with his tongue he went round and round,
swallowing the black and the cold,
separating himself from the race of human beings,
squandering sleep and dreams
in the fellowship of the cold, black winter night.

23. *Spring 1944*

WHEN SHE ARRIVED IN APRIL, HIS CORNER WAS EMPTY. HE HAD ABANDONED
PAINT, BRUSHES, TURPENTINE, SWITCHED TO CHARCOAL. SHE LISTENED TO THE
CHARCOAL SWISH BACK AND FORTH ACROSS PAPER, A NEW SOOTHING, MORE
VOLUMINOUS SOUND, DIFFERENT FROM THE BRISTLES OF THE BRUSH, A SANDLIKE
GESTURE ALONG HER LIMBS, A RAPIDITY, A MOMENTUM, THE GRAVITY OF A LOVE
AFFAIR. HIS HANDS MOVED QUICKER. HE DREW CIRCLES WITH A BLACK STICK,
ABANDONED LINES, HIS ARMS SWEPT GRANDIOSE ARCS. BLACK SMUDGES ON
HIS FACE AND THE TIPS OF HIS FINGERS GAVE HIM THE APPEARANCE OF A BOY.
PATRICE WELCOMED THE CHANGE, BUT AS SUDDENLY AS VERNAL CHANGE CAME,
IT LEFT. IN MAY, THE PAINT AND THE TOXICITY OF LINSEED OIL AND THE RAVENOUS
EYES OF A HUNGRY PRIVATE MAN RETURNED.

May was in its second week. In the morning, there was much of the child
about her, the sash of sateen she wore on her waist, her white shirt
not fully tucked, a grape stain on her sleeve.
She placed a bowl of red grapes on the table
and said, "Why don't you paint this still-life instead?"

The spring afternoon hours passed slowly like a needle mending a hole,
repetitive motions in and out, a weaver of bones.
Louis in his corner with free will, to speak or not to speak.
His silence unbearable, as a candle burning, melting slowly without noise,
inch by inch life pouring out of him.
One day he would extinguish and no one would know.

He dipped a clean brush into the tube of paint, inserted the hairs
as if they were a needle entering a never-before traveled place.
He tugged a string like a magician pulling a scarf and he carried
love-of-white to her face.

Today she craved the company of a woman. The scent of women.
The complaints of women. The turn of the shrew. Women with long hair
and big breasts weeping forlorn. Cheek to cheek, fingers interlaced in dirt
digging for worms they carried to the river to feed the birds, the little wrens.

She tightened the sateen sash around her waist and listened to the sound
of the water rushing from the apartment next door, the woman who cleaned
all day, her dishes, her fruit, her vegetables, her stockings, her brassieres,

her undergarments, her self, the water running, skin oxygenating
and exfoliating until there was nothing left to cleanse.

"Children do not know the meaning of extinction. For children, it does
not exist," Patrice said in her mercurial tone before she closed her eyes.

An hour before sunset she left him and a crisp air from outside swept
across her sleeping-beauty face, an opium of restraint, a muted tinge of
laughter muttered through parted lips. The world was entirely different
from what it had been a minute before.
She became the woman he painted into the bark of his existence.

*He painted her drifting on top of wood, serenaded by violins and strung
lanterns, her face covered with a white scarf. Haunted, he groped and
carved a monsoon of wind . . . then he pulled one loose thread, a secretive
tug not even the pigeons could hear, and formed a thespian mask.*

Toward the testicle of time he interrupted and punished himself for his
desire to kiss and wake her from sleep, for his inscrutable hold of her
leather reins, to ride with her in the conversation with the divine as the
fountain of nymphs outside his open windows spouted waterfalls of truth,
neither rain nor pour, but a modest fall of liquid seething from stone lips,
a hemispheric fall, unearthing his refusal, his blasphemous denial:
I take from her to please only myself.
All the while she slumbered and pretended she worshipped him.

Louis placed his paintbrush down.
"Why stop?" she asked like a child.
"No paint will paint what I see today."
"I am tired of waiting," she said. She lifted her hand to her sateen waist.
"Paint my injury today."

*He fashioned her body in the shape of the Odyssey's prow in the throes
of the wind. A flock of women trekked her body over their heads
through a turbulent sea. Her masked pearly moonface shone like an ingénue.*

A little before six o'clock she rose from the couch and walked to the window.
She looked down at the courtyard and saw Hadrian sitting on the stone
bench beside the fountain of nymphs. The white stone showed its modesty,
the woman's shoulders bare, draped drifts of white cloth like sand dunes

along her torso, the sculptor's tied bow along her fragile waist, her thighs
hidden under more layers and layers of cloth, her feet bare. The woman's
dangerous, frail smile, the folds of her lips, velvet petals opened.
The playful nymphs at her feet, the children consumed in an abundance
of water flowing and filling, never quite spilling over the rim.
The eternal rush of impermanence.

The sculptor's realized dream in the midst of a fever under a starry moon.
The courtyard brimming in lush—a comfortable place with stone benches
for voyeurs to sit, for men like Hadrian in need of a glimpse of modest
nakedness and children in perpetual bath.

24. Summer 1944

PATRICE STOOD EVERY MORNING AND ADMIRED THE BROOKLYN BRIDGE LIKE A DESERTED LONELY TRAVELER STANDING AT THE HORIZON OF THE BARE-BLUE SEA. IT WAS AS IF HER EARS WERE HER EYES, SEARCHING AND SEARCHING FOR A FAMILIAR REFLECTION IN THE CITY'S BELLOWED, HARROWING SOUND. IN THE SUMMER OF NINETEEN HUNDRED FORTY-FOUR, WHEN SHE MET MRS. ITO ON THE METROPOLITAN STAIRS, MRS. ITO REMINDED HER THAT IT WAS DANGEROUS TO LIVE FOR ONE DAY—IT WAS DANGEROUS FOR HADRIAN TO LIVE FOR MONEY, IT WAS DANGEROUS FOR MRS. ITO TO LIVE FOR THE RETURN TO JAPAN, AND IT WAS DANGEROUS FOR PATRICE AND LOUIS TO LIVE FOR THE MUSEUM AND DEATH. IT WAS TIME FOR CHANGE.

The room smelled vaguely of stale art and the sweet warm grip of sleep. The birds assembled outside his window were cooing, and the young girl downstairs played Mozart in the way Patrice remembered from so many years before. Her nostalgic heart beat wildly. She rested her head against the chestnut-wood trim and settled in the pose.

His momentary happiness that had flared up inside him at the sight of her craned neck died as quickly and unexpected as it had come. There must be a limit to mourning for the dead. A sudden stab of sadness filled him with an urgency to begin all over again. He soused his paintbrush in black, and he covered yesterday's mistakes the way others laid coffins in the ground.

He needed air, he could not breathe, he had to keep going, he could not stop. Intersections of black from east to west, from north to south, crossed out yesterday. His paintbrush swept the melancholy of his dark mood across the horizontal plane.

She unraveled herself, straightened her neck, and studied him with intense questioning eyes. She reached out for the bowl and poured clear water over her hands. She raised the rim to her lips and with her tongue she licked the warm water, her throat swallowing the world-weary sorrowed heaviness of sad air.

An onslaught of cold invaded her senses and she covered her body with his blue terrycloth robe. The day was almost over, and the memory of her ten-year-old body returned—she was pressed against the bedroom

door listening to the sounds of her mother begging her father to stop,
her mother crying out for help as Patrice stood frozen and helpless.

"Don't you think we commit to betrayal too early in life?" she asked,
and once it released from her mouth the burden of it dried up the way
blood hardens at the touch of air.

He angled his paintbrush and scumbled black with a downward pull to the
hardwood floor. He stilled a forgotten dreamy existence in the landscape
mounds of her skin as if he were picking the flesh from his very bones.

Spider-black turned that corner of life and death, smearing across the
expanse of his art. He threw his paintbrush to the floor and he smudged her
chest with the heel of his palm. Her eyelids quivered. He breathed her life
into his lungs and brutality black softened. The hardened edges disappeared.
With each inhalation he felt drugged.
The staleness of his art and a vocabulary of darkness and
the unbending summer hours filled him with surrender.

He shut the woman's eyes underneath the magnolia tree. He painted
harvested organs under her tangerine skin, a cocoon of orifices and ovaries
and a discursive vein. Birth. Life. Death. He piled letters at her feet. A stack
of black-ink love scribed to a woman married to love. He stippled apple-red
on her lips. He surrounded the pregnant woman with blackbirds and black
stones and blackberries and black crow feathers strewn on the garden floor.
He blossomed open cupped white and pink tulip petals on the magnolia tree.
To the east, the woman's husband stood at a window. An intellectual man.
A rational spine. A cocked head. Hands clutched a black book.
A red ribbon of blood swam across a baroque mahogany desk.
Silver coins stacked high on the library desk. The face of the grandfather clock
at ten o'clock. Eyes watched his wife read her lover's letters, naked
under the magnolia tree.
A young girl peered from behind the birch tree. Liver-colored cheeks
and yellow pollen rivered through untangled hair.
Cumbrous flesh. Heavy bones. Gauguin bare feet. Frida hips.
Eyes wide open preening her mother's naked body.
The mother's hand reached for her daughter. He gave the mother a gold-backed
pocket mirror. He preened her face. Blushed her cheeks. Combed her hair.
Hadrian would say, shower her in more jewels.
Hadrian would say, give her riches all women deserve.

Hadrian would say, all our mothers deserve more.
Wind from the purple mountain horizon swept past the woman.
Pages strewn. Letters gobbled by red volcanic breath.
He refigured her ear with the blade of his palette knife.
His paintbrush, a silver scalpel in the palm of a steady hand,
painted his circumcision, he a young boy dressed in nautical blue,
his small paw grasping for apron strings, the woman under the shade
of the magnolia tree, her hands clasped to her ears to hide the scream.

Patrice saw the pigeons on the fire escape fly away.
She rose from the couch, and she walked through the cigarette smoke
and placed her hands on the small of his back.

"*Pregnant Woman under the Magnolia Tree,*" she said. "You must name
her in the end. We name our possessions we carry to our death."

25. FALL 1944

PATRICE GAZED OUT THE WINDOW IN SEARCH OF OTHER LIFE-FORMS AND
LISTENED TO THE SOUND OF THE FOUNTAIN OF NYMPHS IN THE COURTYARD
SIPHONING SPRAY. SHE SAW A PILE OF IMAGINARY LEAVES, RED AND ORANGE AND
YELLOW BONES. SHE HEARD THE STRING OF LAUGHTER IN THE STREETS, YOUNG
GIRLS IN A CLUSTER, HAND IN HAND WEARING WHITE MAN-TAILORED SHIRTS
AND PLAID SKIRTS. EVERYTHING MEANT MORE THAN ONE THING. THE END OF
THE DAY WAS NEVER QUITE WHAT SHE EXPECTED. HER SUMMER NARRATIVE
NOW FADED IN THE LAVENDER LEWDNESS OF FALL.

She removed stray hairs from the red velvet couch. The carnal
sickness of the paintbrush clung to his hand. She heard the drip
of his despairing paint.

Cool air seeped through the room and whisked the pincushion of her heart.
She could hear and see the lovely seaside girls who frolicked on the sand,
fingers and toes digging the watermark into earth's soil. She rubbed the
aches in her body. She pinched the tempest of truth in the underflesh of her
arm. Her arm traveled and witnessed, poked fingers in pus and wounds,
carved imprints in mud-caked land, sang nursery rhymes and incantations
of blessings for life, and cornered diggings for death.

He painted over and over again the same part of the canvas. Each single
brushstroke changed what once was. When the work seemed to him to be
at its worst, Hadrian said it was his best. But still he looked at his work
with jaundiced eyes. But still he added the same hue to the same part,
layering skins and skins over a wound. As long as there was the slightest
chance, he had to go on.
He had to keep the paintbrush in constant movement.
He had to paint what he saw.
He blew smoke toward her and said, "So many die in the fall.
So many of us gone."

She hid her fingers and hairs underneath her thighs and she inhaled
his words in the pit of her throat. She watched a leaf inch its way
through a crack in the window. The world outside his window was devoid
of songbirds. She watched the spider leave its cave. It crawled to the same
cadence of the second hand of the grandfather clock. The spider's hoary,
fragile legs crossed the high-vaulted ceiling to the wall, clambered over

the gold frame of her favorite painting and rested in a spot of green like
a woman with a parasol in hand under the shade of a tree. Minutes passed.
The autumnal air was too reminiscenced, the confluence of modern time
side by side the past. She closed her eyes. It was time to leave.

It was September. It was late in the day. They were in their sixth year
and the wax had sealed their edges together. The more time she spent
with him, the more difficult it was to tear herself away from him.
"You paint me, but really it is your own self you mutilate.
You punish only your self," she said.

Later in the afternoon Hadrian entered carrying a wine bottle he placed
on the white tablecloth. The two men stood at the easel and admired
the painting. There was affection between the two men, the way they
stood side by side, careful not to touch, eyes penetrating the flat surface
of her landscape as brothers bound together in inheritance and shame.
Empty words were spoken, and Hadrian showered Louis in praise.
There was affection in the way Hadrian lifted Louis's damaged ego,
the way men spoke about art when you should never have to explain.

Hadrian left the corner like a trained falcon sent from a palace chamber
to deliver a message to a lover hiding in the woods. He sat next to Patrice
on the couch. He flung his arm on the chestnut-wood trim and he inhaled
her lavender scent. She moved closer to him. She inched closer, and yet
they both felt the wind pulling them farther apart.
Hadrian grabbed Patrice's wrist and with his sharp fingernail
etched into her flesh: HE WANTS ME TO MAKE LOVE TO YOU.

*Louis's lips parted in a divine smile. He painted over and over the same part
of the canvas with the heel of his hand. He dug his body into her aorta.
The line of her vein hyphenated. Air seeped through empty slits of an artery.
He smudged life and death in the ventricle of her heart. He pumped his
haughty blue hatred and his childish red love and lunged the deepest sorrow
in her loveliest organ. He kneaded an excursion of romance and ruin, caged
triangles and squares. Shavings and tissues and red autumn leaves foamed
into a red river frothed of velvet blood. He grabbed his smallest paintbrush
and pointed tiny particles, the human eye cannot, must never see.
He dabbed her heart with the sound of waiting for a cup of steamed cold milk
in the night darkness of his ten-year-old room, the sound of his mother
and grandfather in the next room arguing about who his birth father was.*

BOOK THREE

WINTER

26. WINTER 1944

FOR THE LAST FEW DAYS THE CITY BURNISHED THEM WITH THE WORST OF ITS
WEATHER, THE STREETS APPEARED DESERTED AND DEFICIENT, THE SKY VOID OF
BLUE. HOARY FROST CLUNG TO THE WINDOWS LIKE A SPLATTERED KISS. LAPS
OF WATER AGAINST THE SHIPS SMASHED NOISE OF A RUINOUS TIME. A SHIP'S
HORN RANG OUT FROM THE WHARF ENTRENCHING THE CITY WITH A CALL FOR
HELP. A FEW DAYS AFTER HADRIAN BROUGHT GABRIELLE CAMILLE GOTSALL TO
THE METROPOLITAN, LOUIS LOOKED OUT THE WINDOW AND SAW THE RIND OF
THE MOON HANGING OVER THE CITY AS A PERILOUS PALE WARNING. HADRIAN'S
GOOD NEWS WAS FADING. THE PLEASURE OF SELLING THREE OLD PAINTINGS TO
THE RICH PATRONESS OF ART WAS FADING, THE IMPERMANENCE OF PLEASURE
LEAVING ITS INDELIBLE MARK ON THE PAINTER'S PSYCHE.

He tapered her temples with black. Strings of beaded darkness he saved
for the third day when the snow disappeared while the wet remained
in his bones. In the hollow space of his underarms, in his bowels,
a moist potion reminded him of the possibility of dreamy growth.
At any time in the woods, a mushroom of poison could grow.

*The deep shaft within, plunged down, down, and farther down. He shaped
her tones with shadows, distilled atoms he stippled into the cavities
that housed her eyes. He unblended her with a blanket of ghostly visions,
and her lips parted as the chamber of secrets moved deeper down.*

His legs faltered, his knees buckled, and he clung to her face with a
passionate stroke of luck, for he was more inclined to forsake her
face for her arms in the winter months. Her face held his mother.
Her face contained Vienna. Her winter face forfeited her own life
for his fantasy of the past, that romantic Cupid arrow he brought
out during the aftermath of snow when the purity of white
had annihilated his palette of charmed hearts.

"Very little exists outside of us," she whispered from the red velvet couch.

His infirmity, his weakness when he listened to her near-perfect words,
led him to the cliff he hid in the landscape of her lips.
For days he had contemplated the sheer simplicity of jumping
from the edge, but she anchored him in her sea of blood.
She held out the veins of her wrist, and she tempted him with

the choice of death. The fall of snow enlivened him
with the will to live, and her still lingering masculine scent
kept him in accord with their mirrored existence.

Very little, it was true, existed outside of them and yet they were both
hungry for the invitation, to leave the room and step outside in the biting
cold, for the wet seeped through the cracks in the wall and flooded them
with the thought that one day the end might be near.

He advanced deeper, the shaft within him pounded palpitations, coursed
through him as he lit a cigarette and blew the benign smoke her way.

She inhaled it. She held it in her mouth and she swallowed it in her throat
and he stroked her temples with sable hairs, his bristles tap-tapping
the only black angles he had implanted on her face, for she was elliptical,
an oval round of divine beauty he refused to line with lies.

She raised her head and she looked at him. Her deep ground eyes
fixed on him a serene fright of distrust. The snow had awakened her
lack of faith, and December's cruelness harbored her discreet disdain.
Doubt rose from her skin like tiny silver needles. Her eyes threaded
a cocoon of hide-and-seek. "Paint me even more beautiful today,"
she uttered out loud.

He reached for his cigarette. He remembered his conversation
with the Patroness of Art as she looked at the paintings of Patrice.
Gabrielle Camille Gotsall had said, "I must have her."
"She is not for sale," Louis had said.
"Name your price."
"She is mine. She is not for sale."
"Don't be foolish Louis. Let us learn to share."
"I've not finished her yet."
"You can paint more."
"You can buy her from Hadrian when I die."

He returned to her temples. He opened the skin, and peeled the layers
of yesterday's paint and he collaged a brass key beside her pink brain
and stitched the sliced flesh with invisible cat-gut thread.
He inhaled his cigarette and turned her temple door into hourglass shapes,
the sound of snow in pebbles of sand.

Patrice begged him with the wave of her hand, and he blew more smcke in her direction.

"When you sew me back together again, when you refuse to sell me like a piece of property, you make me beautiful and warm," Patrice said.

27. *Spring 1945*

APRIL IN NEW YORK CITY WAS A WARM WELCOME MONTH, DAYS FILLED
WITH ILLUSION, MORE LIGHT LASTING LONGER THAN BEFORE, CITY STREETS
GLISTENING SPECKLED DIAMOND LIGHT, NIGHTS LOUDER AND REVERBERATING
DESIRE AND EXPECTATION. CROWDS OF PEOPLE SURFACED, FROM WHERE,
NO ONE WAS CERTAIN. FLOWERS AND DWARFED TREES PLANTED IN TERRA-
COTTA POTS, CLOSE TO THE SUN ON ROOFTOPS, BLOOMED PARADISE-GREEN.
VENDORS SPREAD BUSHELS OF STRAWBERRIES AND ROWS OF SILVER SALMON
ON CRATED SHELVES. INSECTS TRYING TO ESCAPE, DRAWN TO THE LIGHT,
DIED GALLANT DEATHS AGAINST WINDOWPANES. CHILDREN COUNTED THE
DAYS UNTIL SCHOOL WOULD END. WINTER CLOTHES WERE BOXED AND TAPED,
GLOVES AND SCARVES PUSHED TO THE REAR IN DRAWERS, BOOTS DISCARDED.
SEAMSTRESSES ABANDONED BLACK AND NAVY THREADS. CLOTHES WERE
PINNED ON LINES TO DRY. MUSICIANS FORGED INTO THE STREETS. AN ARTIST
DREW ON A SKYSCRAPER WALL A PASTEL IMPRESSIONIST PICTURE OF A WOMAN.
RELIGIOUS ZEALOTS PASSED OUT FLYERS PROMISING REDEMPTION, HOW TO
AVOID ETERNAL DAMNATION. BANKERS APPLAUDED LOWER INTEREST RATES.
HINGES WERE LUBRICATED. FLOWER SHOPS WERE FILLED WITH DAFFODILS AND
GLADIOLUS AND IRISES AND TULIPS AND VIOLETS. A SLEW OF BABIES WERE
BORN IN MRS. ITO'S HOSPITAL'S MATERNITY WARD. PATRICE AND MRS. ITO MET
ON THE METROPOLITAN STAIRS LIKE A PAIR OF WIND-UP STARLINGS, WELCOMING
APRIL'S RETURN TO A FRACTURED CITY IN NEED OF REPAIR.

But Patrice was too good a model to be adventurous. She stayed herself,
committed her mind and body to the eerie spring air, its soft gentle touch
on her flesh, dragonfly wings fluttering for a place to rest.
Her thoughts were cleansed with the promise of renewal of weather's turn,
and yet she felt a stab of envy, his feet stepping on the hardwood floor
as she held herself contained in a container of hidden-ness, dismissing
the desire to inebriate her being with enticingly unknown adventure.
For if she were to wave her arms in a frenzy symphony, if she were
to exercise her freedom and pounce from the red velvet couch
into his turpentine-infested painterly arms, he would punish her
with those cold, cruel words reminiscent of winter and he would
admonish her and quell her and push her away, far away.

Her heart was good. Her heart filled with tenderness.
Today she loved both the good and the ugly as she harnessed her
body in spring's wound-up pose, her tensile muscles clenched to

her bones in that preferred staid and still-life way
that impassioned painters in spring.

Grains of pollen drifted between them, the color of yellow,
the smell of sex, the scent of unbridled mating.
She held back her sneeze, heaved in a mouthful
of fluids, and shifted her pelvic floor into the red velvet cushions
keeping her vow, keeping her innards tamed to his art.

She was good but it was harsh, to be so innately good but so unhappy
with the fractious parts, her whole ensconced in his pastel-spring paints,
her myriad parts diminishing as she held her strength to his wishes—
for adventure was a pornographic word in his lexicon of nonfiction,
and she was instructed to behave, to be good, to hold still,
to not move, to avoid provocative movements of both arms
and legs that disturbed his concentration.

"You are an original form," he said.
She reminded him for the third time, "The original is a volcanic
explosion never to be harnessed again."

*An interlude. The silence was broken. His whimsical self surged as he sloshed
his paintbrush into cadmium's cool yellow and crossed from his palette
to canvas, carrying the scent of nectar to the corners of her eyes to enlighten
the good in her deep, mineral-rich brown eyes with the vibrant stroke
of distinguished adventure. Her irises emboldened with excursion.*

Her unhappiness faded as she watched him paint her goodness.
Her eyelids weakened and she slowly closed her eyes. Her arm around
his waist led him subdued in her überhold.

"The original is always the best."
Louis dabbed his paintbrush in a mound of blue.
"You think I am original because I am unchanged from day to day."
Patrice opened her eyes.

"No two paintings are the same." Thick Paris blue hung to his fingernails
as a remnant of winter's hoary frost clinging to a leaf. "No two paintings
are the same," Louis said again, louder, more pronounced, as quicksilver
frothing from the lips of an undefeated man.

28. Summer 1945

ON AUGUST SIX, NINETEEN HUNDRED FORTY-FIVE, THE UNITED STATES DROPPED
THE ATOM BOMB ON HIROSHIMA. SEVENTY THOUSAND PEOPLE WERE KILLED,
AND SIXTY PERCENT OF THE CITY WAS WIPED OUT. MRS. ITO GRIEVED FOR THE
INNOCENTS WHO DIED. SHE MOURNED FOR HER HOMELAND. SHE IMAGINED
MR. ITO STILL ALIVE INTERPRETING THE WORDS OF TWO NATIONS TOWARD
COMPASSION AND PEACE. SHE IMAGINED HER BELOVED HUSBAND STOPPING THE
MADNESS OF REVENGE LOST IN TRANSLATION. ON THE STAIRS, MRS. ITO TOLD
PATRICE: MAN IS THE ONLY ANIMAL THAT PREMEDITATES TO KILL ITS OWN KIND.
EACH ONE DEAD IS A MILLION DEAD.

A young moon was out. Outside they killed each other with fire
and the fountain of nymphs sprayed her waterfall of innocence.
The sound of splash and the smell of youth mused the room and Patrice
lay on the sandybeached red velvet couch, harboring the storm of the
weary-world, the warehouse slaughter of the poor, the mushroomed
explosive pincushion of atomic energy dropped on Hiroshima.

She turned from Louis as one might shut out a trespassed man.
She bent her head to take in the one lonely pigeon begging for bread,
and she smiled at the moon.
For a slim moment she delighted in herself born a woman.

"Today, you must paint me as if it were the first time. As if it were
the first and only time." She closed her eyes and lowered her head.

At the speed of thunderbolts he smeared eggblue across her belly.
The whole scene an unforgettable splendor both excited and frightened him.
The paint became dense, thickened and sickened with stretch marks.
Her body born an accessory, first he etched a thorn and then a blue
bewitched rose. Her navel he rounded into a blue barbaric globe.
Time's ruins building eternity's relics. Her face held the pose of a Greek
goddess found in lost caves. Above her head he carved an old-fashioned
yellow parasol. He fractured the shade. In the foreground he beaded yellow
petals on paved stones. Carriage wheels carting a cannon, glistened like a
chariot of fire. His heart pounded like a warrior, his paintbrush spear in hand,
relentlessly battling the murderous day.

The young moon farther out. She asked for a glass of Hadrian's dry red wine.

He dropped his paintbrush in the glass jar. Like a crane standing ashore, he looked at the old-fashioned parasol suspended in the sky.

He strolled past the pigeon on the fire escape flapping its pink-and-blue wings, past the couch, past her seasalt smell to the table. He clasped the green bottle and raised it to his lips and swallowed. The wet of his shirt stuck to his back ribs. He poured her a glass and tiptoed to the couch.

The moon farther up and gone. She reached out, clutched the stem and held it in her shaking hands. "We will get drunk," she said. "Drink to the death of your civilization."

Later in the day, for a moment he felt as though he could delay his own death. The mysterious obstacle vanquished. The news of the atom bomb meant art mattered. She was no longer his model. She was the shared fate of all. She was refunded in silence. Her mournful lips were sealed. A violent spasm awakened his reverie.
He maneuvered the hairs of his bristles into an empty hole.

He pulled his eyes from her mouth and traversed like a wanderer without food and clothes through the deep, desolate forest of growth. He cleaved to the small opening at her heart. He painted the rim copper. He gave her a metallic armor. Her enemies abound, he shielded her in one of Mrs. Ito's paper fans, her oppressed hands hidden and chained under her thighs. Her copper heart pulsated with mined riches. He harnessed her with an iron girdle to hold back her emotions.

She lifted her chin and cried out, "No better vision waits for you but this one. Today, you must master the paint. You will no longer paint your self in my face. You will paint our hurt."

He exacted a few more brushstrokes. He erased blame. He steadied his hand, and he carried the now bronze-tipped brush to the eastern corner where he lay to rest his primal flaw. Her bare foot a mound of succulent meat, a handmaid's paw, in the valley of the reeds, waiting for the color of war to fade. He painted her toenail the color of a bronze coin and with his fingernail he scratched Hadrian's profile into the veneer. He left a part of himself bedded to her confessional foot.

He had failed, he could not stop from leaving his mark.
The curvature of her embrace, the style in which he painted her legs and
her arms entwined to gnarled roots of a tree, tore open her copper heart
of love as he rotated the globe of barbaric blue on its axis.

Far away, distant and detached, she whispered, "Men might learn to love
were it not for their obsessive nature to love love."

The pigeon flew away, and the young girl downstairs pounded on her
piano keys.

He felt a sensation rush over him. His knees weakened toward the
hardwood floor. He lifted his paintbrush in the air, his wrist hovered
as a brood of pigeons begged for more bread. Wings flapped a continuum,
a vague unrest, yet he held to himself, lowered his hand, stabbed his
yellow-tipped bristles into a well of violet as if he were diving his body
into her heated heart.

Louis lost a charm with every breath, a desire to end what he had begun,
a fear of losing the originality of his newfound hue. He had dreamt it at night,
with Hadrian pressed to his back. He had loosened Hadrian's fingers
from his neck, in the same way he dug sand on the beach. The memory of
purple enslaved his horizon, transported him to the red cave. He offered
Hadrian a wing from a slaughtered bird, as if he had defeathered himself.

The hue held like her summer tears. A cocoon of wetness safely confined
in a silken web. Love that might have been. His hands felt for the opulent,
played for the experience, unearthed the cave-red rock and flung
a streak of violet in the northernmost corner of the canvas with the
timid graceful lashing, a violent moment of pleasure.

Her eyelids quivered. She sensed his anger. She, too, longed to please
and condemn. To bring him the perfect hue she harbored in her locked
belly berth, but today she was without. The atomic mushroomed city
plagued her vision and she was without.

"We are guilty," Patrice said in the voice of a foreign woman.

His hand trembled, flailed to the east and the west, a pendulum motion,
an arc of prehistoric time surfacing tiny threads, texturing a purple circle
over her garland hair. He swept back and forth, combing the curls away,
farther and farther away. The yellow parasol shined like the sun. The paper
fan glowed like a moon. Smoke rose from the barrel of the cannon.

"When we die, they will say we did nothing," she whispered into the August
air. "When we die, they will not pay us any attention." He shuttered her out.

Lost, she shifted toward the edge of the couch. Her hand underneath her
thigh held her up. Her eyes peered beyond his drenched back at the fountain
of nymphs. She postured her chest in his direction, heaved her unused arm
over her head to the nape of her neck where she pinched her flesh to enliven
her throat with the comfort of silence.

The grandfather clock chimed four times. How accurate the sound was.
It heralded the time of day when the heavy weight of the day lifted and
her body stretched and smoothed its aches along the red velvet as if she
were slipping through a secretive passage only visible to discerning eyes.

Surprisingly at these revealing moments, he planted the subtle shade
of green into the canvas as if he were beginning the start of a new garden,
acutely aware of the power of the sun and the fluidity of his paints,
keeping them in a liquid state.

How strange it was his desire to grow, to root himself in the flawed
and fractured parts of her body, to drench her soil with the thickest
nutrients. The finest and most linear lines he drew in the dying hours of
the summer, for the end of the season was near, the autumn would come,
its intelligence and its rebirth, a new seed of insurgence, all helpless men
and women in the city craved.

She listened to the caress of the river and she pleaded with him.
Her hip moved. A slight gesture. A silent understanding passed
between them in the heartening memory of imagination,
for both were certain the painting he painted on this particular day
was praiseworthy and bound to be remembered.

The fissured threads of her roots and the climbing branches
of her arms and her curls of hair, all of it, every pigment of it,
a vision of all things that are to transpire, all things in the past
and all things in the strange rare moment when the woman looked
at the man and waves of remorse invaded her, and she felt unclean
for she knew their time together must expire.

The privilege of her loneliness, her uncleanliness, her frigid
movement of a hip during the bombed summer,
perhaps it was morbid, perhaps it was guilt.
In absence of understanding, she imbued his colors with brilliance,
she heaved her pains heaped on pains, and her hidden thoughts,
her authentic self rose bearing a composed smile of bitterness.

Perhaps he loved her smile, perhaps he preferred the folds of her lips.
Her morose mood subsided, and the afternoon light turned that corner
of darkness, and the spider on the high-vaulted ceiling crawled down
toward the hardwood floor, and she waited patiently and carefully for him
to place his paintbrushes in the glass jar and sit beside her on the couch.

There in the room they stilled themselves in the aftermath of art.
He wiped his hands on his thighs, cleaned his skin of her,
and she solemnly waited.
The mystery of what might follow, what might not come penetrated
the space between them. The recurring sound of the river and the sound
of the city preparing to close its doors, kept them close together in this
strange moment of love for the intimate private thoughts of another.

How strange it was that she had somehow predicted this—
you do not have to understand a man in order to love him.
"Breathing room in pain is all too brief," she said.
"We must share our hurt. We must not rage on forever . . ."

29. FALL 1945

AS HARD AS THEY TRIED TO CARRY ON IN THE WORLD AS IF NOTHING HAD HAPPENED, AFTER THE BOMBING OF HIROSHIMA, LOUIS, PATRICE, HADRIAN, AND MRS. ITO MADE A PACT: THE FUTURE OF CIVILIZATION RESIDED IN ART. AS LONG AS ARTWORKS WERE BORN THE WORLD WOULD CHANGE. IN A CLOUD OF SECRECY, LOUIS MADE LEGAL PREPARATIONS FOR HADRIAN TO INHERIT HIS PAINTINGS WHEN HE DIED, AND PATRICE MET WITH THE PATRONESS OF ART TO SET THE GROUNDWORK FOR THE RECOGNITION OF LOUIS'S ART. IN THE FALL OF NINETEEN HUNDRED FORTY-FIVE WHEN THE DEATHS OF LOUIS'S MOTHER, FATHER, AND GRANDFATHER WERE CONFIRMED, FEARING THAT LOUIS WOULD DESTROY HIS PAINTINGS, LOUIS AND HADRIAN AGREED THAT HADRIAN MUST STORE THE PORTRAITS OF PATRICE IN THE BASEMENT OF THE WHITE RABBIT CAFÉ. WISHING TO RETURN TO JAPAN AND NURSE HIROSHIMA'S BOMB VICTIMS, MRS. ITO VISITED THE BURN PATIENTS AT HER HOSPITAL. HER ACUPUNCTURE NEEDLES RELIEVED THEM OF PAIN. SHE WROTE HER TEACHER TO SEND MORE NEEDLES AND BEGGED HIM TO SEND HER THE OIL FOR ONE OF HER SPECIAL PATIENTS IN DESPERATE NEED. SHE WROTE: MY WORK IN THIS COUNTRY HAS REACHED THE END OF ITS COURSE. I HAVE MET A WOMAN AND TOGETHER WE CARVED THE PATH YOU INSTILLED IN ME. PLEASE MAKE THE NECESSARY ARRANGEMENTS TO BRING ME HOME.

They were to stay like this for many days. The light from the window
neither black nor white but grey, autumn's first hue asunder stealing
the vibrancy of summer's warm tones. The air was crisp, abruptly smearing
its war cries on the skin of both the painter and the model, to remind them
of nature's inscrutable joy of defeating the highness of comfort, to keep
them realistic and lonesome, in sway with the natural course of earth.

It was the young girls Patrice remembered, their innocence and
the way they once moved along lawns of grass and cobblestones
of long undulating fortressed city avenues in the mansions of time.
The days of the young were gone, withered in the annals of the war
as autumn reminded her and spoke to her in that cool voice,
the brisk voice of a widowed woman who perhaps had lived
too much of life or breathed too much of death.
Patrice was to stay like this for many days,
fleetingly remembering the young girls, their toes
slipping in sand as they stood before their masters,
victims in a ring of fire, their guardians in deep denial

of the true nature of family love.

The gravity enjoined them in a morose mood. The birds of paradise in
the vase, the orange and purple and brute blue, tethered day by day,
grew in the autumnal air.
In a room full of rich artistic minerals and materials, the chemistry of the
flower and the atoms of the water and the crystal-clear gleam of the vase
glass in which the stems stood grounded Louis and Patrice like landed
warplanes after fleeing threatening enemies.
And the paint on the canvas clung and gripped like cells anxious to defend
against cancerous souls of humans consumed by self-pity and self-hate.

They were to stay like this for many days, in this menacing state
each waiting for the other to exercise freedom, for the scales weighted
down to be lifted up, each waiting for a collision of his imaginative skills
and her aged powers to form the laborious expression they waited for
in the aftermath of the war.

It was extraordinary. They would wait and wait and wade through the grey
and mine the remnants of the visible world between them as a woman and
a man in lust of art.

Around her strode shapes of fear, his fearful eyes
that looked but did not observe and refused
to penetrate the limitations of his paints.
Patrice knew it would take more, more ammunition and more blood
and more deaths for the painter to bore his way through the trappings
of his fragile manly body and open the virtues of art's vow.

She broke the silence. "Nothing in nature is without purpose.
We must protect the earth that feeds and rears us all."

The heart inside him fired up as he listened to her words as he mended
her broken bones with the orchid-pink mixture he had concocted earlier
in the day when he waited patiently for her arrival, watching for her
out the window, seeing the first autumn leaf rolling down the street.
The melancholy of red, the melodic twirl of red,
the microscopic motherly love of one red leaf,
a perfect, not too much and not too little hue
he turned from red to pastel-pink.

30. WINTER 1945

AT NIGHT THE WILDEST ABERRATIONS OF THE CITY UNFURLED AS A HIBERNATORY
ANIMAL DUG OUT OF WINTER EARTH TO STRETCH, TO BREATHE, TO SIPHON
THE INTERCOURSE OF WILD LAUGHTER ON THE DARK-RIMMED STREETS, A
TIME-DULLED CHAIN OF NIGHT'S OPIATE, ITS RAKED LABYRINTH OF SEXUALITY.
IN THE NIMBLE WINTER MORNING OF NINETEEN HUNDRED FORTY-FIVE, SHIPS
SOUNDED HORNS OF INDIFFERENCE ALONGSIDE THE JINGLE-JANGLE OF SNOW.
THE SNOW FELL ON THE CITY AS SHOVELED DIRT THROWN ON A GRAVE. PIPES
FROZE AND THE TIME IT TOOK PATRICE TO WALK TO THE METROPOLITAN AND
THE TIME IT TOOK LOUIS TO BOIL WATER INCREASED. FOG ESCAPED FROM
THEIR LIPS WHEN THEY SPOKE AND ICE FLOWERS ON THE WINDOWPANES CLUNG
IN A DESPERATE ACT OF BLOOM. OUTSIDE, THE SMELL OF CHESTNUTS WAFTED IN
THE AIR, SMALL FIRES BURNING ON EACH BAROQUE WINTER CITY CORNER, MEN
IN WOOL COATS AND GLOVES SERVING FOOD TO THE CITY'S FOOLS.

In the keep of his walls he found himself in a winter reservoir of stillness,
standing on the other end of the world. The biting cold outside clashed
against his windows, the inhabitants of the city waking to life with
the first subway quaking underneath.
Embankments of snow obliterated the avenues and a valley of microscopic
white vanquished the intersections, erased any trails of existence.
He inhaled his cigarette and blew smoke across the room
in her direction.

He steeped his paintbrush in emerald-green and dabbed the contours of her
hips with the finest glints imaginable in December, when time drained from his
veins in small pools. He flushed pale streaks in the panorama of sky he had
arranged methodically and patiently yesterday when the first blush of snow fell.
He smeared a razorous plane. Cloudbanks sharpened and stretched with the
blade of his palette knife. He thought woman is truth, and he scalloped
the thought in the sky's rough edges. He formed a buttress of light
funneled through the puffs of clouds. A dawn-broached sky filled him
with a sense of survival, a desire to remain a painter in the swallows
of winter's cruel breath. He smeared a faultless sky and the calamitous
advance of a yellow sun showered her hips with an eerie glow.

His insides smiled and his painting hand tremored, his fingers one
at a time opened and the paintbrush fell to the hardwood floor,
winter's fury resounding in the keep of his walls.

All the while she slept curled like a December cat under his blue
terrycloth robe. She scaffolded her thoughts one on top of the other,
and her foundation quaked and crumbled, each part fell to the bottom,
gashing the conduits of her cranium. Already it was as if he never existed.
So early she was a hibernatory animal, burrowed underneath all alone.

She rebuilt her thoughts. It was the only thing worth painting—
she felt more immensely and more lovingly every day. It was her heart
and her soul—the only thing worth painting. She opened her mouth
and a haloed fog of breath drifted toward his direction.

"Why must you continue to paint the outside?" she asked in a stern voice.

He bent to the hardwood floor and lifted his paintbrush in the air.
He walked to the couch. He caressed her head with the back of his hand.
He touched her with the tender purr of art. Heat from his hand
warmed her surface skin, while inside she remained stone-cold.

She whispered in his ear, "As long as you continue to paint the outside cold
you will never conceive the present, the inside, the now."

31. Spring 1946

IN THE SPRING OF NINETEEN HUNDRED FORTY-SIX, NEW YORK CITY BORE THE WASTE OF THE LAND, PAPER STREWN ALONG ITS STREETS, MOTHERS CRYING OUT FOR THEIR CHILDREN DEAD IN THE WAR. PATRICE PASSED BY THE GUARDIANS OF THE CITY SITTING ON BROWNSTONE STEPS. THE WOMEN, THE EYEGLASS OF THE WORLD, GATHERED AND GOSSIPED, STAYED HOME AND RAISED THEIR YOUNG, KEPT THE GUTTERS CLEAN, THE SIDEWALKS SAFE, PROTECTED THE STREETS. THE WOMEN SET OUT THEIR WARES, ESTABLISHED THEIR TURF ON THE STEPS. THEY READ, ATE, TOLD STORIES, STRETCHED, STOOD TO PEER, SHADED THEIR EYES, COUNTED THEIR BLESSINGS, THEIR MONEY, THEIR WOES, THEIR HAIRS. LIKE STATUES MADE OF STONE, CARVED BY MEN TO PROTECT THE CITY WALLS, THE WOMEN SAT ON TOP OF THE STEPS AND REPENTED FOR MAN'S SINS.

A queer thought clung to Patrice as she crossed the threshold. If she gave too much, she would kill him. She placed the brown-paper bag on the table, and she undressed with the motions of a child afraid to show nakedness to a stranger. If she pretended he was a foreigner, if she feigned their connection, she could hold back a piece for herself, a morsel turning deep inside, the kernel of truth she kept locked in captive moments.

Today, she had awakened with a new sense of freedom, her bones
an armature of lovely bones, her fractures mended in the war-torn
evening hours as she slept alone in her uneventful bed.
She carried a piece of the newfound freedom in the brown-paper bag,
beside succulent fruit she had chosen from the market merchant who
eyed her with that tremulous deep burning inside, fierce hateful eyes,
so eager for a piece to claim as his own.
The taste of freedom lay next to the green and violet grapes,
like a lonesome charm ready to be opened and sucked by Louis's
childish lips, for in the first month of spring, Louis clung to his fantasy
of me, of mine, of possession, and longed for his dark shadows to fade
while she conspired to keep the hidden to herself.

She straightened her weakened shoulders, and she walked to the red velvet
couch and fell to the cushions like a prisoner released from years of captivity.
She slid the paper under the pillows,
pushed the secret deep into the crack
and quelled her queer thought as she rubbed
her tongue along the cone of her wet lips.

He seemed to welcome this, to applaud the early morning gesture
and her submissive silence. He lifted his paintbrush and doused it
in yellow and honeyed his pollinated bristles along her throat.

If she loved him too much, she would kill him.
If she granted him his most desired wish, she would destroy him.
If she opened the cavern and spilled her blood, he would suck
and drink and drown in her sorrow.
Instead, with dignified grace she curved her elbow
in the shape of a question mark and she closed her eyes
and dried her lips, swallowing her fluids as he spread and
defined her shape into mounds of yellow blossomed petals,
a bouquet of flowers waiting for more sun and more rain
in desperate need of an admirer's eyes.

Her world-weariness seeped from her pores and the sound of his
paintbrush turned that violent corner, resonated with thunder-clap.
She inched her elbow farther out, over the edge of the red velvet,
she gave him the inquiry, required him to examine her body parts
with the eyes of a physician anxious to save a patient from death.
For surely she would die, it was time to die, she, too, was tired of living,
of giving, of breathing, of posing womanliness.
Her elbow ached with the death-wish,
her lovely bones turned into madness, angry bones
desirous of revenge, victim bones hungering for freedom.

She opened her eyes and the brown-paper bag was gone.
He could not help himself. His curiosity raged.
He had abandoned his travels with yellow and opened the bag.

All the while Louis feasted on the grapes, Patrice smiled.
Her insides asssembled.
The code lay safe in the confines of the red velvet.
The code was indecipherable to a stranger.
The code clung to her queer thought.
The code was secretive and only available to the chosen few.
She smiled as she excluded him from her circle of friends.
The guardians of the city packed their wares,
left the steps, went home—
and the women on the walls laughed and

an encore of applause exploded in the room—
and Franz, his master returned.

The old painter hovered by the window and admired the yellow painting.
She was exquisite. It was modern. The painting was a brilliant expression.
Its genius the pain of memory. It answered a question. Franz had loved
Louis's mother and loved being Louis's teacher and had killed his student's
imagination. Louis's new teacher, Patrice, loved him in a mythic way.

32. Summer 1946

PATRICE WALKED TO THE METROPOLITAN. THE DARKNESS IN HER DIMMED. THE
HEAVINESS TO HER GAIT A SMALL DIN ON PAVEMENT, THE SOUND OF THE STREET
DIN AN EERIE DESOLATE ECHO. THE WORLD WAS ENTIRELY CHANGED AS AFTER
A STORM WHEN THE WEAKEST, THE WEAKEST CHILDREN AND ELDERS DIE. SHE
WORE ON HER FACE A CULTURAL MALAISE OF A DEATH OF A PEOPLE. SHE LOOKED
AT THE BROOKLYN BRIDGE AND REMEMBERED IT WAS THEIR SEVENTH SUMMER
TOGETHER. SHE WALKED THROUGH THE AVENUES AND THE STREETS TOWARD
THEIR TIME TOGETHER TO REMAKE THEMSELVES IN A DECAYING WORLD. IN THE
HABIT OF THEIR WORK SOMETHING BLISSFUL WAS BOUND TO COME.

He felt a million miles away from Vienna. Vienna still came to him
during mornings when she was late. When Louis felt abandoned
he remembered prolonging his breath while being smuggled out
of Vienna in the coffin his grandfather had built.
He remembered pretending he was a clock without gears.

The summer morning was fragrant with lemons. The pigeons jealously
waited on the fire escape expecting an offering. Louis snuffed his paintbrush
in grey and studied the monotone, a perfect blend of black and white
he smoothed while anticipating Patrice's arrival. It was a mythic color,
one he imagined the ancients had blended in times of sorrow.
When he began with drab grey it meant the day
would end with an onslaught of heightened colors,
the landscape redressed with a multitude of brightness.
A shaft of light shot through the windows, and the color grey
cried out for even more cosmic elements.
He ailed with desire to return home to Vienna.
With a flick of his wrist, he blocked the light, shut out the intensity.

She entered the room wearing her sadcolored face. She lay on the couch
sheared of life. "If men are so potent, then why do you kill other men?"
she asked during the first minutes they spent together.

The tendons in his arms tightened. He could not take his eyes off of her.
"Survival," he muttered out loud as he carried the grey matter
to the easternmost corner of the canvas, a precious open space
where anything surreal could happen. "Raging impotence
drives monsters and men to kill."

She squirmed, contorted her body as if convulsed by a slow-dying poison,
and then she thrust her being into his psyche. He could always feel
when she disapproved of his color choice. As much as he told himself
he was the painter, he was in control, she was the commanding one.
The conversation with the woman was her narrative, not his.

"Men fear what they do not know, what they do not have." A tinge of sighed
relief escaped from her mouth. "Men rob our bodies when given the chance."

She rose from the couch and limped as if he had painted her hip
socket away. The couch kept the forever-warm impress of her body
as if she never left. She moved the vase of gladiolus on the table
so that she could see his face when she spoke.
She walked to the grandfather clock.

He watched her press her ear to its heavyweight chest, listening
to a heart of a pregnant woman carrying a child.

"Your grandfather was an exceptional artisan. His clock will outlive us both."

He walked to the grandfather clock, put his ear next to hers
and listened to the heart murmur. Golden brass wheels spun
inviting him into the antechamber of time.

Later in the afternoon, Louis served her the bittersweet virgin
lemonade he had prepared in the morning. They swallowed slowly,
quietly quenching their thirst, neither vulnerable nor afraid. He grabbed
a handful of ice cubes and wiped his temples, his cheeks, and his chin.
He wrapped ice in a towel and pressed the bundled ice on her wrist.
She laughed out loud. He rubbed the towel along her shoulders,
down her rib cage, hips, and legs.

"Don't stop," she said. "Finish what you have become."

33. FALL 1946

IN THE FALL, ON A NAKED NOVEMBER DAY, THERE WAS A TRAIL OF SEDIMENT AND SENTIMENT THAT EXISTED BETWEEN THEM. LIKE A MARRIED COUPLE, A TRAIL OF DUST ONE REFUSED TO CLEAN. THEY, WOMAN AND MAN, RESIDED IN A PERPETUAL STATE OF COMPLACENCY. AND YET, BOTH LOUIS AND PATRICE WERE PLOTTING TO QUICKEN THE PACE TOWARD THE END.

The painting of Patrice gave something of the illusion of passage.
The paint like dust had settled thick on it. Journey loomed in the mist.
The mysterious unknown, the somberness of fate,
the harrowing corridor of the unexplored.
She was at the center of the universe, her tranquil anatomy
and the marrow of her bone a shade of undying breathlessness
the human eye traveled terrain to mine.

Deep in peace, she slept. Deep in solitude she slept, while Louis gripped
his paintbrush and showered the illusion with reality, desirous to nourish
the shadows of her anatomy with the strength of a woman
he had come to uphold in the fantasy of his time.
Oblivious, soft, and warm sleep surfaced across her eyes.
A mere brushstroke of light swept the canvas cleansing
the armature of her existence with the science of art,
their exalted reason for being.

It was unreal in a way, how he thought she was deep in sleep,
when really she was living and breathing, traveling through the volcanic
ruptures of time, legs stepping and climbing, her body rising toward the sky
while she felt herself a stake driven deeper into the red velvet couch,
her body sinking closer to earth, her mind and her eyes repairing
the ancestral relationships of time.

She felt his paintbrush along her flesh, and she welcomed
his precise calculations, the way he balanced the reddest red
with the darkest black, his mastery of paints, an alchemy of creation,
his ability to make art out of dust, his determination to be a sane man
who refused to go mad.

"How on earth can wounded men continue to go on?" she whispered
from the caverns of sleep.

The painting turned that corner and gave something of the illusion
of courage, brave wisps of paint pounded the surface. He dabbed her body
with the color of flirtation. A blotch of yellow ascended to a band of orange,
the color of distilled ambrosia. He covered her naked humiliation
with a seasonal robe, a pile of leaves, edges carved and cut like exact stencils.
He opened her maw, and she swallowed the waves and gulped out a plume
of seafoam. He raced with the waves and swelled her veins with strength.
The sun's rays intersected and divided the painting in three parts.
The fertile sun seeded him. The threadbare time and the second hand of speed
and the advance of light hurried him. He marveled at the perfect perspective,
the lost vantage point of time. How easily he forgot where he began.
How easily he dressed her in a blanket of leaves in the month of November
before the onslaught of unbearable cold when earth began her sojourn
down into the depths of her soul.

She would soon wake from sleep. She would open her eyes
and he would stand in the corner with the painting,
his paintbrush dangling in his hands as he studied his mistakes.
He would assure himself that tomorrow would come
and all might be different and completion was near,
tomorrow each lonesome part would intimately grow
the way lovers formed a union under leafed cloth.

34. WINTER 1946

WINTER MONTHS IN NEW YORK CITY MADE PATRICE FEEL LIKE A MINIATURE
IN AN OVERSIZED WORLD OF STEEL AND GLASS. A COLD HUNGER SETTLED
IN HER BONES AS SHE WALKED TO THE METROPOLITAN THROUGH THE SNOW
PAST SMOKESTACKS AND SMOKESTACKS. MRS. ITO GREETED HER ON THE STAIRS.
HER FACE SMOOTH AS A RIVER ROCK, BROKE OUT IN A KIND NURSELY SMILE.
MRS. ITO HAD DONE THE UNFORGIVABLE, SHE HAD FALLEN IN LOVE WITH A DYING
HOSPITAL PATIENT, DONE THE MISTAKABLE, HAD FALLEN IN LOVE WITH A MAN
WHO WAS DESTINED TO DIE, YET ANOTHER MAN WHO NEEDED HER BY HIS SIDE.
MRS ITO HELD PATRICE'S HAND AND TOLD HER: ONE CANNOT QUESTION ANOTHER
MAN'S LIFE. WHY MUST WE ASSUME WE ALL CLING TO THE SAME DREAM? LOUIS
IS READY TO DIE. HADRIAN IS READY FOR LOUIS TO DIE. YOU ARE THE ONLY ONE
PROLONGING HIS WISH.

In the vault of his world, a tinge of remorse, as if he had never seen
this before. The red embedded in her eyes shined radiant stars of
elegant stones, mined impressions he had carried across the Atlantic,
rubies his grandfather had wrapped in his mother's white handkerchief
stained with her operatic tears.

He bit into the bread, held the crumbs in his mouth, tasted the salt,
the bitterness of blessed bread. He ignored the affection and
the compassionate wintery stare Patrice brought from the vault
of the cold into his steam-spitting piped heated room.
He floured her red eyes with a swipe of pure white.
The harsh thrust of snow falling outside
the window kept her even more inward,
kept her a prisoner to the couch,
as if he had never seen this before,
a woman lying so close to the edge of death.

And then her hands crept from her abdomen to her neck, fingers
crawling like thin spider überlegs so compassed in need of a place
of safe isolation away from openness, her hands seeking refuge
from the rise and fall of her stomach, seeking a woman's neck
like a smooth-sanded coffin of rest.

"Your thoughts are morbid today," she said as her hands reached
their destination and tightened her veins.

He was accustomed to this pose, the holding of the neck in its most upright,
the way a woman wore a necklace of rubies to enliven the blood to the heart
and brain.

Her hands were void of red, both a Shakespearean and Elizabethan moment
in time when Victorian darkness of love reigned in the terror of repressed
love. But he was committed to white, to the white bread that settled in his
throat as he swallowed the crumbs and widened and sharpened her eyes
with eternal white ice.

"You must unmake this cold world you cling to today," she said.
Her words like a chained chord pulled and heaved him once again
across meters of ocean, waves of swelled impressions.

But the bread tasted good. The loaf she carried into the room in the month
of February was a perfect composition of water and flour and yeast and salt.
He stippled grains of pebbled white in rapid successions,
tap-tap-tapping more white under her eyes to hide the
ruby-red jewels only he and Hadrian knew were smuggled
across the ocean in the chest of a clock in a coffin.

"We all live at the level of truth we cling to," she said, the coarseness
of her tone audible, the pout of her mouth succinct.

35. *Spring 1947*

BOTH LOUIS AND PATRICE FOUND IT DIFFICULT TO SAY FAREWELL. IN THE
SPRING OF NINETEEN HUNDRED FORTY-SEVEN WHEN PATRICE ARRIVED AT THE
METROPOLITAN, LOUIS SULKED IN HIS CORNER LIKE A CHILD. AFTER PATRICE
UNDRESSED AND LAY ON THE RED VELVET COUCH HE SAID: I WANT TO BE BURIED
IN THE GROUND. WEAR YOUR BLACK AND YELLOW DRESS. LET THEM WITNESS
YOU AS I FIRST SAW YOU IN THE WHITE RABBIT CAFÉ. AND PIN A RED ROSE WITH
ONLY ONE THORN IN YOUR HAIR.

The modern-ness of the day smacked of antiquity and ruins.
The air that carried him breath by slow breath across the hardwood floor
was turning lusciously like an escort. He stood in silence—the canvas
had become as dense as the inside of a crimson red rose.
His eyes drawn to the center, hovered on the periphery,
on the edge of disappearance. His shirt stuck to his back.

More sinned against than sinning, she covered herself in modesty,
cloaked herself in humility. Her olive arms crossed at her chest.
In the folds of the rose she was alone. In the pressed petals of blood,
she was invisible to the world.

He stood before the near-finished canvas—he was so unused to feeling
a sense of survival among her ruins.

"There is no more left to paint," she whispered. "We are done.
You have reached the end."

The air shimmered with gold and violet queenly ribbons as the words
poured and thrust from her mouth, so authoritative and all-knowing.

He shuddered. His shirt peeled from the flesh of his back.
"I am not done with you yet."
"You finished me months ago, but you continue to persist," she shrilled
in the voice of a woman at odds with the weather and the sea looming
aloneness of communal spring.

Secretly, inside he bowed to her words.
But his hand flung from his thigh to the
paintbrush standing erect in the glass jar.

Secretly, he mourned his impotence,
his inability to create without destruction.

Secretly, he wished to erase the delicate red lace, the intricate edges
he scribed into the landscape of each one hundred petals.
Secretly, he wished to tell her how he embedded the invisible vague
veneer of her face into each of the one hundred red rose petals.

The rose bride drifted through the desuetude.
Her gold and violet robe swept the hardwood floor
with the sound of a waterwave. A knife was wedged
under her sash, should the rose bride change her
mind in the early morning after her wedding night.

He clenched his lips, and he clutched the wood handle as if
it were the key to unlocking her impenetrable chained door.

"Isn't it enough that I let you enter once? Why must you desire
to return, time after time, when there is nothing left to give?"

36. Summer 1947

THE LAIR TREMBLED LIKE THE WILLFULNESS OF A CHILD. THE CAVE, HER DEN PATRICE HAD COME TO KNOW AS HOME, FORFEITED MORSELS OF TEARS. THE VELVET COUCH, WITH ITS LION'S PAWS TREBLED A DEEP ROAR. WHAT WOULD THE AFTERNOON BRING? WOULD ANOTHER PIECE OF HER SOUL BE SHAVEN AWAY, THE PALETTE KNIFE COLD AND BITTER AGAINST HER FLESH? WHY MUST LOUIS STAND POSED IN A PAINTERLY STARE, THE ONSLAUGHT OF A SMIRK ON HIS POPPY-COLORED LIPS, WHILE HER EARS RADAR INTO THE SOUND OF THE LAIR'S ROAR UNABLE TO MAKE IT STOP? WHY MUST THE PAINTER PAINT ONLY WITH HIS EYES, NOT HIS EARS?

There in the room, she lay in awe. Stricken with wonder, she exploded
in the rarity of the cloudbanks about to break. The noise dissolved as
she watched the white puffs hover over the buildings in that pristine way
nature held its sway over creatures.
It filled her with a sense of order and proportion, the leveled
field of equality that reigned in her never-ending present life.
The grandfather clock chimed its elusive charm and its black hands
moved, breaking across her flesh, awakening her from her stupor.

He looked ugly. He stood in his corner, intent on himself, eating a feast
of Cancerian foods, as he did in the early days of June, when he crawled
into his shell anchored on land, away from the fluidity of water.
She smelled his strawberries, and she felt the coarseness of the seeds
lingering in his throat, his lust for fruit, his enchantment of feeding his art,
nursing his body with sweet roots, embroiling his images with hues
of spring colors brightened and more brilliant in the month of June.

She paddled her thoughts.
She rowed herself to a farther place, a faraway island of reeds,
the whirr of captured stalks caressed by a subtle summer wind.
She pushed out farther away into the belly and bowels of a man-made lake.
She sensed how he strengthened the cords of her muscles,
felt him standing ashore, sketching her insides with brightness
and brilliance, instilling her flat surface with manly strength.

They enjoyed each other's company.
He was ugly, but she pleasured herself with his labors, the way
he diligently magnified the sinews and threads of her flesh.

An insurgence of new blood swelled her veins, and she loved him for
a brief moment as she turned a corner and paddled away from him.

Contentment surged when she gave in to his whims and
then went on her way like a young girl turning from a god.
Tender was her smile and rapid was her retreat.
She reeled deep into his paints, arched her neck,
and flew through the broken clouds, soared like a phoenix,
left his nest of ugliness and discontent,
his sorry art imprisoned there in the room.

"I am your inheritance," she said.

Overhead, she watched him squirm, watched his fear turn to anger,
watched his paintbrush swirl in his left hand, watched him reach
for his long-forgotten cigarette burning in the ceramic ashtray,
watched him hunt for her like a young boy looking up at the sky
for the string of a yellow balloon.

She turned aster yellow, and from above she handed him strawberry red.
More words came to her. It was too late. Time expunged the memory
and words failed to perfect the order, the perfect proportion.
Her awe, his fear smeared the veneer of the canvas
in a way one hundred years from this day,
in the time of romance and remembrance,
two strangers standing in the museum
famished only for passion on a Junian summer day
would look on the body of a naked woman
in the troublous confines of a woman's time,
her guardians of passion watching and safely protecting
the future of strangers amid the first time of life.

"We should sacrifice something of yours that causes you anguish," she said.

37. FALL 1947

ON THE STREETS ON THE WAY TO THE METROPOLITAN, PATRICE WAS AWARE OF
FOLLOWING FOOTSTEPS ALONG HER TRAIL, FOLLOWING EYES WATCHING AND
WEIGHING HER EVERY MOVE. SHE STOPPED TO ADMIRE THE BROOKLYN BRIDGE.
AFTER FIVE HUNDRED YEARS POSING NUDE FOR PAINTERS SHE WAS FATIGUED.
AFTER EIGHT YEARS WITH LOUIS SHE WAS TIRED OF LYING PASSIVELY ON THE
RED VELVET COUCH. IT WAS TIME FOR LIFE'S PLEASURE TO BE BORN AND ALL
PAST SORROWS TO DIE. THE SPAN OF THE BRIDGE AND THE COILED WIRES
SHE HAD CLIMBED AND CLUNG TO LIKE A SPIDER IN ITS WEB ON THAT FIRST
SUMMER NIGHT IN NEW YORK CITY, REMINDED HER THAT IT WAS NOW TIME
TO LEAP FROM CONTINENT TO CONTINENT.

Cast afresh in the morning, placid Patrice lay on the red velvet
couch in the Neptunian seminal air, her underlip curled out.
Holding on to the chestnut-wood trim she ground herself in the delicious
delirium of Phoenician purple the painter smeared on her neck.
Her serpentine-tongue muttered the words, "You burn me," and her staunch
blossoms unfolded to the rhythm of his waterwave, that sensuous sound
of bristle hairs stroking the flat surface and the tap-tap-tapping of his
left black shoe to the hardwood floor.

The salt-sting of the planet enamored her senses, for men were greedy—
yes they were—and the woof of the red velvet pressed against her
autumnal skin as she slipped, slid, swooned down to the soft membrane
of her forever-without existence.

The expression of her lip, turned toward that moored mysterious
moment in time when the painter stopped and laid down his brush
and walked to the couch to implant a kiss on her cheek. Gratitude
for the touch and the reprieve, she watched him fetch his last cigarette,
and the pigeons outside his window flapped their unfettered wings,
and she awaited his catlike footsteps inching down The Metropolitan
stairs as he journeyed into the world to fetch her a bottle of red wine,
cheese, bread, and a handful of succulent grapes.

Her spine stretched out and beyond and her toes hung over the edge,
all the while she charmed herself and giggled at the thought that he trusted
her to be alone in the confines of the walls, among the walls of women who
whispered and spun tales about him while he was gone.

Her foot touched the hardwood floor and she leapt to the corner
with the intention of perfecting her portrait. She looked out the window
and saw Louis standing on the corner with his last cigarette between
his third and fourth finger.
The traffic light turned red, and he appeared not to notice.
On the street he looked like he might fall off the curb, or a car, or a wind,
or a stranger could in one quick moment knock him down.

She turned her back to the window and dipped his brush in the Phoenician
purple and her wrist hovered close to her waist, her breath purring lonesome
imprisonment, her autumn-apricot eyes studying the landscape of her body,
a flattened horizon of Elysian plains.

At first she was serene as she fixed his lines, as she added intelligence
to her expression, as she parted her underlip with Phoenician purple,
as she breathed life under the mounds of her breasts.
And then the women on the walls cried out a bedrock of plainsong truth,
and she painted her madness, a rope tightening her throat.

She heard his footsteps returning, a slow pace up the stairs. She reversed
back to the couch, to the eternal pose of boredom and submission, and hid
her purple-stained hands secretly underneath her thighs.

At the end of the laborious fall day, during the orange hour
along tops of glass, along skyscrapers, along the pier, she asked,
"Would you like something to drink?"
"Water would be good."

She strolled to the refrigerator and poured him a glass of cold milk instead.
She walked to the couch, watched him gulp the milk down.
He placed the empty glass on the table, kneeled between her legs,
fell between her knees, lay between her thighs, and she removed
the paintbrush from his clenched bloodless hand.

She held the shellacked wood handle, and she imagined shoving
the bristles in his mouth, pushing and plunging the hairs
between his teeth into his gums, stabbing and stabbing him
with her love, gathering the blood that gushed from his mouth,
carrying it home in a glass jar, dipping her nib in the red,
writing her own strident story on a white vellum page.

He fell asleep.
His cold, milky breath dribbled along her thighs.
She ran her fingers through his moist black hair,
rolled him to his side,
covered him with the blue terrycloth robe,
slipped into her pants, shirt, and shoes and
walked home under the burnt-orange sky.

38. WINTER 1947

AT NIGHT LOUIS WALKED TO THE CEMETERY TO FIND A TOMBSTONE TO CLAIM
AS HIS MOTHER AND FATHER AND GRANDFATHER'S STONE. THE IRON GATE
CREAKED. HIS SHOES SANK IN THE SNOW. A PATH DESIGNED BY A MASTERMIND.
A MONKLIKE GRAVEDIGGER TENDED THE GROUNDS. LOUIS CARRIED A STONE
AND A DRAWING IN HIS POCKET, FLOWERS IN HIS HANDS. A DOG BARKED AND
WAGGED HIS TAIL. THE ANGEL OF DEATH EXPOSED HER TEETH, BECKONED LOUIS
WITH SNARLING TONGUE, AND HE PLACED THE STONE AND DRAWING BY HER
FEET. BENT DOWN ON HIS KNEES, HIS HEAD BOWED TO THE GROUND. HE DUG
THROUGH THE SNOW AND LIFTED A BLADE OF GRASS TO HIS NOSE, INHALED
THE GREEN, ATE THE GRASS LIKE A DOG. HE LOOKED FOR PRISTINE LIKE A
WANDERING FOOL SICK WITH LOVE. HE GAVE HER OFFERINGS, FLOWERS AT HER
FEET, FLOWERS IN HER VASE, GIFTS HE THOUGHT WOULD REUNITE HIM WITH HIS
FAMILY IN THE WORLD TO COME AND WOULD BRING HIM CLOSER INSIDE PATRICE.

He angled his head away from the canvas and looked out the window.
She held her head against the white sheeted wind. How easily Patrice
traipsed through the snow, her footprints deep wells, her hair tied to her
composed skull, how easily Patrice fell and spread her arms and her legs
in the snow, pretended she was the angel of fallen children.
White snow clung to the lips of the fountain of nymphs.
He studied the silenced sculpted smile.
The rest of the city, snow-white falling, disappeared.
He peered from the grey-eyed statue to the ambient light
of his paint.

Two hours later Patrice lay immobile.
There was not a soul about, besides them.
Her eyes surveyed the surface of his dressed body, only the flesh
of his hands, his grave and sober face, and neck were exposed.
She kept her eyes from meeting his eyes, held him at the
needed distance, kept him from abandoning the painting,
kept him swollen with art.

"Paint me the color of an angel," she whispered in the tenderloin of cold.
She heaved her breastbone toward the ceiling and gave him her
pearous pose, the one she saved now for the coldest moment of
winter, the one full of her strident voice, the voluptuous one she
gave that rounded her edges.

"Don't paint my thoughts today. Paint my winter heart.
It's time for you to begin to paint our farewell."

In the hive of her hair he painted her angelic face and jabbed her with
Mrs. Ito's black lacquered chopsticks. His fingernails combed stray strands.
He wet her lips with the imprint of his palm and cupped her undying calls
into a half-moon smile. His violet-tipped brush lingered at her throat, edged
a shadow of regal hope and flecks of mirrored winter snow. He grafted violet
from her throat and spawned a romantic face and strung lights of a fantasy in
the hive of her hair like a tree in a park. Tears roiled down her violet cheeks.
He painted her pink-blushed heart, barnacles crusted to infinite nerves,
a system of infinite red threads. His paints riffed a percussion of beating
drums, his lack of understanding, his need to know. Threads turned to liquid,
the heat of the heart, molten lava, wondrous animal love. He dug his
fingernail between the coral stitches sewn to her heart.

"I exist only for those who wish to live on," she said, pressing her lips
into the crack, separating the secrets she penned in the red velvet couch.

The whole of New York City unrolled on either side of her, its captivating
crowds milling back and forth, a reservoir of disquieting calm, women
and men traveling toward the future distance, away from the past,
a disturbing pulsation of figures delivered from place to place,
an alarming noise of doors opening and shutting, wheels spinning,
tales embellishing winter-white truths, prolonging death's decaying toll,
a downpour of snow wiping away the unknown.

39. *Spring 1948*

LOUIS WALKED UPTOWN TO THE MUSEUM. HE SAT ON THE STEPS AND WATCHED THE CROWD ENTER AND LEAVE. IT WAS IMPOSSIBLE TO FEEL WHAT IT MIGHT BE LIKE. A WORLD WHERE HIS PAINTINGS HUNG IN THE MUSEUM WHILE HE WAS GONE. HE DETESTED THIS WORLD THAT REFUSED TO HANG HIS PAINTINGS IN THE MUSEUM WHILE HE LIVED. WHORLS OF CIGARETTE SMOKE HOVERED ABOVE HIM IN HIS SEQUESTERED CORNER ON THE MUSEUM STEPS. IT WAS IMPOSSIBLE TO KNOW WHY HIS WILL TO SURVIVE DRAGGED ON AND ON. IT WAS IMPOSSIBLE TO PREDICT THE OUTCOME. EVEN IN HIS DEATH HE IMAGINED HE WOULD SMOKE. EVEN IN HIS DEATH HE IMAGINED HE WOULD HOLD HIS VIENNESE PAINTBRUSHES IN HIS HANDS. EVEN IN HIS DEATH HE IMAGINED HE WOULD PAINT WOMEN, NOT MEN. THE AIR OUTSIDE THE MUSEUM HELD A DISTANT REMOTENESS. HE LOOKED AT THE EMPTY SALLOW FACES OF THE CITY CROWD. IT WAS STRANGE HOW COLOR CAME AND LEFT AT THE MOST UNEXPECTED TIME. IT WAS STRANGE HOW COLOR DREW HIM AND PATRICE TOGETHER LIKE THE MAKINGS OF THE UNIVERSE. IT WAS STRANGE HOW THE SEASONS WHEELED AND SPUN. STRANGELY TOO, HE SAT BEFORE THE MUSEUM AND FELT IT WAS IMPOSSIBLE TO PAINT WHAT HE SAW. HE PRIED HIMSELF FROM THE MUSEUM STEPS AND WALKED TOWARD THE METROPOLITAN DETERMINED TO LEAVE A LUSTROUS AND SUMPTUOUS TRAIL OF HIS EXISTENCE.

It was exactly twelve o'clock. Louis and Patrice stayed like this,
an adoption of a long moment. The air filled their lungs
as if the metabolism between them instilled a fusion.
The moment slowed down, stayed and stilled itself to dense
matter, a heavy weight of existence they both clamored for
during their seemingly last months together.

They claimed each other's eyes, an adoption of inner thoughts,
for now the words between them were empty. They had experienced
it all, all the pains and joys of human nature. In the Taurus air, their
sexes stood firm, any hope of lovemaking gone, touch dwindled to a
back or a neck.

Mounting minute by minute the paint on the canvas dried alongside
the heat. The temperature affected his hues, the dourness of the heat
imbued his colors with emotions. It marveled him how The Metropolitan
absorbed the sun's radiance, how he lived in the most desirable haven
of New York. Such good fortune to live so far away from the museum.

Louis placed his paintbrush in the glass jar on the three-legged table,
and he walked to the couch. Her hair fell about her face, and she removed
the strands from her mouth. He fanned her with his palm, careful not to
touch, and he studied her expression. Today she was a bouquet of purple—
lavender and violet shimmered on her skin like a Viennese glassblown vase.

He saw his own reflection in her curves,
a dark shadow of human nature usurping her hues,
in need of vision and image, for the end was near,
he was certain, as those near to their own death
desire to be alone.

Her eyelids quivered, and he stepped back to the canvas.
He lifted the paintbrush from the turpentine jar and blasted it in red.

"No more red," she said. "Paint me yellow, the color of the verdict
of human nature."

But he was intent on replication and repetition, his rhetoric of paint,
the image, the object, the color. The grandfather clock moved forward.
He carried the image of her violet and lavender face to the canvas,
a metaphor for his soon dying days.

The late April air shifted as the noon light turned that inevitable corner,
a high peak climbing down the rungs of survival, for even the sun
could not withstand its own powerful intensity,
its impenetrable enchantment among human nature,
even the sun wished to cover himself up and hide
from the power of her moon.

And so he cleaned his paintbrush with a rag and jabbed the hairs
into a well of cadmium yellow and stippled periods of pointed matter
along her poetic elliptical mouth.

40. Summer 1948

THE SUMMER AIR FILLED HIM WITH AN AVALANCHE OF SENSATIONS. A DAMP
MOISTNESS HUNG AND FOILED THE CITY WITH FALSE PRECIPITATION AS IF IT
MIGHT RAIN IN THE MOST UNEXPECTED MONTH OF THE YEAR. THE CITY SEEMED
SEALED, THE INHABITANTS MIGRATED ON, ONLY LOUIS AND PATRICE LEFT TO
FINISH WHAT THEY BEGAN.

The air was tonic with distrust. Ether crawled up his spine. He placed
his paintbrush between his thumb and index finger and penned his most
interior thoughts into her skull. He had spent the morning blossoming
her cranium, tinting a cluster of earthworms. Yesterday he had fattened her
with water, injected fluids inside her muscles, tendons, and skeletal bones.
Then he had covered her with the folds of a white shirt, dressed her torso
with the hands of a servant. He hovered for a moment and swept the
bristles in a downward stroke of gravity that filled him with surprise.

He was drawn from her brain to the left side of her white shirt.
He was possessed now by another new and even more truthful thought.
He had blamed her for everything.
There seemed so little movement in the world outside his window
as he groveled with playful apologies he hoped to shower her with
after he settled in the cushioned confines of her heart.
He had not touched the organ in days.

 "You're like an actor," she said. "You make believe that your character
loves and is apologetic for his mistakes."

He placed his paintbrush down and stubbed out his forgotten burning cigarette.
He lifted the palette knife in the air, and he tore the left side of her white shirt.
He cut an incision across her heart slowly and kindly, careful not to slice her skin.
The cool metal in his hand turned warm. Her constitution, her face amid
the first time of life, vanquished his sad airs. His life stretched before him.
He heard the sound of dragonflies atop his most favorite Viennese lake.
He stippled the hole of the shirt with grey. He darkened the color with the
queer properties of black.

She arched her neck. She sank to the velvet, her body a summer weight
of a flower consumed by the sun. She pulled farther and farther
away from him in the darkest hour of distrust. It was poisonous.

The way they danced together in the final minutes before
noon, the least hour to bear, the hour he would leave her.

She waited for him to step back.
Men were greedy, so they were, she thought as she anticipated
his departure to fetch her melons from the outside world.

The feverish pelting sun needled her skin. Patrice flirted with the sun.
She remembered at night her mother sat and sewed. She remembered
watching her mother's stoic complexion. Her mother thread the needle
with her eyes closed, her feet flat on the floor, her body still except for
the hand that held the needle moving in and out of fabric. Patrice listened
to her breath, the sweetness of her mother's night breath that swept the
room, as if her father and her brother and Patrice gathered to watch and
inhale her mother's mood. No one dared to break the silence.

Patrice sat at her mother's feet and read. Her father sat in his chair and
read too. Eyes moving across the page, the sound of thread and needle
through cloth, the tick-tock of the clock, the fire cackling in the stone
fireplace, the dog breathing and dreaming in her sleep, the silence of
the family together under lock and key, dinner settling down deep in
their bellies, the sound of night trees outside the window, shadows
dancing across the walls, ghosts escalating in the room.

She raised herself from the couch. The red velvet peeled from her skin.
She walked demurely across the hardwood floor. Her arm reached
out for his most favorite paintbrush. She inserted it in a well of red.

Men were greedy, so they were, she thought as she looked at the painting
of a woman. She mended her heart, fixed his mistakes, his erroneous
perceptions about trust between a woman and a man. She stretched
the lining of her heart, turned the walls vibrant with the emotions that
swelled inside her.

He looked at her painting she had done of his. He blared his eyes.
It was as if she had rifled through his innards. He blotted out the sun
with his hands, blinded his eyes and breathed in the scent of cantaloupe

still lingering in the flats of his hands. She had captured the first inhalation
and the last exhalation, completed the painting with the finest lines,
invisible intersections joined the parts into a decipherable whole.
She had finished herself, lurched her imagination in marriage with his
divorced self, melded a wondrous union lacking his crack of discord.

He treaded on the verge, his muscles drawing into his bones,
all of him desperate to regain control, sucking toward the heart,
his core disbelief in his own work rising to the surface with each
waking breath, his lack of worth in the summer month when heat
robbed him of his confidence.
She had lumbered through his possessions in the way captives turn captor.
She had pilfered his interpretation of the meaning of life,
his religion now smeared with her love,
her evolving birth and her beautified deification.

He removed his hands from his eyes and walked to the couch and covered
her mouth with his palm. Her legs moved like two fins swimming upstream.
Her stomach rose and fell and he listened to her murmurs for help.
He bent over her and breathed on her.
His throat was dry, the sweetness of the orange melon
long gone the way fleetly pleasure came and left him.

"I know," he whispered. "I know what you do when I am gone."

She nodded her head in complicity, a pulsation of agreement.
She understood, her mouth still in his hand a mute testimony
of shared secrecy. She nodded yes, turned that corner of woman to child,
scared of punishment, desirous only of love.

Yoked together, a couple of malady, the sickness between them nourished
the art. He saw it in the way the women on the walls watched the drama,
lamented and moaned. He heard it in the way the city forgot the plot,
closed its doors to a woman and a man drowning in a room on one sultry
summer day in the Americas. He tasted it in the way Patrice ran her tongue
along his fingers, neither biting him nor gnawing at his strength.

She lay calm and still, defiant and tender. Slowly, it righted itself.
Politely, her violation ritualized itself. She had painted the end.
She had coined the stoppage of time. She had fused the gap. She had rifled

his possessions, killed his weaknesses, murdered his perfection,
added a woman's touch, portended the portrait with passion's arrests,
erased his sex, and filled his paints with a flood of amniotic waters.
He cried like a child and one finger at a time left her lips.

"When you leave me alone, I grow to love you more," she said. "Don't you
think when we are finally apart, we will love each other more?"

He straightened his spine and glided from the couch to his corner.
He grabbed his paintbrush in his left hand and stippled the lines
of her mouth with spider-black.

Death was a matter of importance, but it could wait. June's sun
pierced his back and sweat roiled from his underarms to his waist
the way sugar traveled down his throat, unabashed and fearless
of the descent. He ladled the honey-colored copper he had prepared
while she had fixed herself in the bathroom after lunch. (He was
never quite sure what feats she performed behind the locked door.
He imagined her standing before the mirror with unquestioning faith.)

He carried the copper hue to her collarbone and nestled in the cavity.
He painted slowly. He told himself not to hurry. He slowly caressed
the lineations of her bones as if he were climbing—each sweep
deliberate—on the edge—careful not to fall into the constraints
of order and proportion, for death could wait as he made love
to her mysterious ways.

The sound of the half-hour died away. Her fiber and muscles were
his to own in the summer months when she let down her guard.
The physics of copper turned that corner when the pigments
feasted, and her flesh turned aglow.

He corseted her chest, threaded her lace, tightened her skin,
flattened her face, and her eyelids quivered that moment in her time
when time no longer mattered and she settled in the pillowy red velvet.

She was benign.

His death was important, but she, too, desired to delay
the hour of his end until the painting was completed.
She reached for the glass of red wine.
She held the stem between her fingers and said,
"Nothing in my mystery is to be despised."

He entered her heart. The copper fused with yesterday's red blood,
and he muttered apologies for yesterday's mistakes and he inserted
his paintbrush, a needle through her valve.
Like oil and water, the sensation of order and proportion returned,
but he was anxious to move swift and far away from the chorus
of order and immerse himself in the painstakingly slow motion of
unearthing her heartbeat only known to her.
He slowly spread the bristles like the wings of a bird, and tranquil
with the universe, he slowly stroked and feathered her heart with copper,
zinc, and magnesium and he slowly penetrated the ramrod of her soul
and he slowly entrailed the essence of her soul with his manly venom
and he slowly tortured her with the greatness of his art and he slowly
wired the order with copper's alchemy and he slowly seethed in the folds
of her heart the balance of his hate and he slowly etched with his nail the
hour of his death and he slowly stitched her main artery with ebony-black
crosshatches of time and he slowly returned to his childhood of play and
he slowly embedded their hours and years together in the most secreted
organ he could find, all the while she slept, her breasts moving up and down,
drunken wave after wave.

She was benign and he was malignant, but in his death he would
return as a woman.

June came to an end. Morning turned to afternoon. Patrice had arrived late.
Life threw up wreckage, and a new landscape opened before him. He plumed
his sable hairs in violet vellum and he circle-swiped her radiant cheeks with
saturnine rings. Yesterday's paint eroded as a galaxy of new sullen rays
spiraled her feminine charm.

She was an enigma. Her elasticity in the summer months collided
with his desire for order, and the wreckage she had carried into the room

kept him akin to his intention, for he was close to his death and summer
would turn its naïve childlike corner and burn his body into ashes and dust.

She was narcissistic, in love with love of the self, and no matter how
hard he penetrated her cheeks with violet's violent stream, no matter
how he warred with her not-of-this-world fixed smile, she questioned
why he lingered when they were so close to the end.

Her smile reminded him of an ancient fresco found in a hidden cave,
her lips curved in a sex of a different kind. His paintbrush steady
in his left hand forfeited his intention, abandoned his order. He fled
from her smile to her neck and nestled in the curvature of her bones,
a place where he hid when he was terribly afraid. There were women
and there were women, and violet's echo of "I love you" filled him
with urgency to feast on purple's undying pigments, and so he licked
his tongue, infected his mouth with turpentine's smell, intoxicated his
saliva with tormented thirst and he obviated her neck, a sever not even
the human eye could see. Yesterday's paints flooded with fluids, her
main artery cut by the precise hands of an artist so close to his death.

Her smile turned at the corners. Wistful and hopeful she whispered,
"When you are done we will drink to the birth of your babes."

Bereaved, old, and frail, his wrist turned limp, and he looked into
the silver-cinched band of his paintbrush. He saw his own reflection
in the mirror and his eyes pulled away and he looked at the grandfather
clock and saw his image in the androgynous face, and he turned away
and glimpsed at the wreckage. Her stalked neck now hung drooping
like an iris in a glass vase, and he saw his own tired, terrible child, his lost
face embedded in Patrice's anatomy, for all along he had been painting
his self-portrait in the veneer of her face, his manliness and her feminine
symphony of violet's romantic reds and brute blues.

He heard noise outside his window. City life now bustled with summery
couples, women and men in twos, paired together by the fate of lineage
and seeds. The Junian air drifted past him. He swallowed the pool of toxins
he held in his mouth. He tore himself from the painting, and he looked at her
sleeping-beauty face. He was greedy, so he was, and not one hundred years
from now, but only one thousand years from now, they would find the day
he had sliced her neck.

She uttered a whisper through the lips of her smile, so soft he inched
forward, "Why must you linger when we are so close to the end?"

The grandfather struck five o'clock. His paintbrush poked the cavity
of her heart. His hand as steady as a surgeon, invaded the canal.
Violet blossomed red-blood, his hairs spread and fanned, and he
swam through the corridors of her most treasured organ.

Her heart was not his to own. There were women and there were women,
but the woman that lay on the red velvet couch, her aristocratic name,
Patrice, the patrician, and the paints, his memory, his deep reverence for art,
nothing would ever imitate her.

He lit a cigarette with a somber match, and he stepped back from the easel
and studied her red heart, a petal-closed rose, never to be plucked again
by a venomous man.

41. FALL 1948

IN THE FALL OF NINETEEN HUNDRED AND FORTY-EIGHT, PATRICE AGAINST THE MANDATE OF HER GODS, INFUSED LOUIS WITH THE POWERFUL MAKINGS OF ART SHE HAD KEPT FROM THE OTHER PAINTERS FOR FIVE HUNDRED YEARS. THE TWENTIETH-CENTURY WORLD WAS ONLY READY FOR THE PAINTINGS OF WOMEN THAT WERE CREATED BY A MAN. EACH DAY SHE OPENED HER HEART, SHE FOUGHT THE WRATH OF HER GODS. ONCE SHE CHANGED THE FATE OF ART, SHE COULD NOT STOP. ONE OCTOBER NIGHT, WHILE ALONE AT THE WHITE RABBIT CAFÉ, HADRIAN DRANK JUST ENOUGH WINE TO REMEMBER LOUIS'S WORDS: THIS PAINTING IS FOR YOU. WHEN I DIE, I DO NOT WANT THEM TO SAY I NEVER PAINTED A MAN. HADRIAN REMOVED THE PAINTING OF PATRICE HANGING OVER THE MAHOGANY BAR. HE POURED TURPENTINE ON A RAG. HE WIPED HER FACE SLOWLY AS HE HAD WIPED AWAY DUST FROM CHRIST'S FACE WHEN HE WAS AN ALTAR BOY. THE COLOR OF THE AZURE MEDITERRANEAN SEA SPREAD THROUGH THE THREADS OF THE WHITE COTTON RAG. HADRIAN DRANK JUST ENOUGH WINE TO SEE HIS IDOL THE PRIEST AND JESUS' BLUE EYES FOAMING IN HIS HANDS, AS IF CHRIST HAD FINALLY COME IN THE END TO SAVE HIM AND FORGIVE HIM FOR HIS SEXUAL TRANSGRESSIONS WITH THE PRIEST. HADRIAN DRANK JUST ENOUGH WINE TO SEE THAT UNDER PATRICE'S PORTRAIT LOUIS HAD PAINTED HADRIAN AS A PERFECT, UNFLAWED HANDSOME MAN IN EARLY NOVEMBER, MRS. ITO RETURNED FROM JAPAN. SHE HAD DISPERSED HER HUSBAND'S ASHES IN HIROSHIMA AT THE GARDENS AND TEMPLE THAT HELD IMPORTANCE TO THEM WHEN THEY WERE CHILDREN. MRS. ITO HAD MET WITH HER TEACHER, AND HE GAVE HER A GLASS PHIAL. SHE SMUGGLED IT OUT OF JAPAN SEWED INSIDE A SILK KIMONO SLEEVE. MRS. ITO HAD ARRANGED TO HAVE TEA WITH HER HUSBAND'S FRIENDS, BUT THEY SENT HER AN APOLOGETIC NOTE. SHE KNOCKED ON THEIR DOORS, BUT THEY REFUSED TO OPEN THEM. SHE LEFT JAPAN WITH A PANG OF DISGRACE. ON THE SHIP'S RETURN TO NEW YORK CITY, MRS. ITO HAD MET A YOUNG JAPANESE MAN WHO ADMIRED HER HUSBAND'S WORK. EVERY NIGHT HE CAME TO HER CABIN. SHE WORE HER KIMONO AND RECITED MR. ITO'S POETRY, AND THEY MADE LOVE TO EACH OTHER ON THE OCEAN.

And, of course, Patrice loved life boundlessly, the soft moments of time that escalated into fantasy and fiction and the mundane dullness that surged the everyday. She loved life, the here and the now, the chaos of autumn leaves, colors exploding and wiping out the bareness of desolate winter.

Life itself, every moment of it, every drop of it simmered through her bones

as she freely gave him entrance in, as he painted the interior of her heart
with the pulse of a delicate balance, fine bristle hairs unearthing the
fractures and fissures of her most favored organ, the red and blue mass
of capillaries, a conduit to her unravaged mind.

Life itself, every moment of it, every drop of it was lofty, the weight of objects
gone, the gravitational pull of the day-world gone, the foreign, the mystery,
the unexpected reigning, encrusting, and enlivening her love of life,
her forgiveness, her goodness.

The visitants, winged messengers from the underworld, lounged on
the chestnut-wood trim of the red velvet couch as if stopping by a pool
of water to stave off thirst, so eager to taunt the painter, to inflict fear
into the steadiness of his hand, while she settled in the natural pose
of a woman, pleasuring herself by the touch of his bristles.

She arched her neck, strengthened her muscles, let him catch the thrust
and the pull of a woman helping a man, her ribs expanding as her lungs
breathed the newfound autumn air, a blossoming magnolia scent that
commanded her to abandon the visitants, to ignore them, to concentrate
on the painter's desire to penetrate her heart and her soul and her harbored
desire to be a decent woman.

Life itself, every moment of it, every drop of it, was entrenched in sound.
The swish-swipe of persimmon red, his most prominent color of her heart
and the aggravated stipple of spider-black, the darkest dark.

Her face turned into marble whiteness and the wind of it, the absolute
absence of words, kept her strong and decent, kept her neck arched
in an upright position, her throat dry, her eyes sweet, her fingers pressing
deep into the red velvet. The hierarchy of objects, the sweeter the better,
the classical the loftier, the silence the bitter, red chronicle of time.

Men were greedy, men were selfish, yes they were, she thought
as she gave of herself so freely, so willingly, letting the painter roam
like a free man through the caverns of her inner wisdom.

The visitants, the gods, watched every moment of it, every drop of it,
life draining from her as the painter pilfered her secrets,
unlocked her shame, his paintbrush bristles altering the terrain,

combing her heart's walls with the eyes of a woman.
Five hundred years slowly quietly politely leaving her body.

Her eyelids quivered, and she fell into a deep sleep, falling into a pile
of chaotic autumn leaves, the white marbleness of her face, stone-cold.

42. WINTER 1948

IN THE MORNING LOUIS PEERED OUT HIS WINDOW AT THE LIVERED EMPTY SKY. THE CITY LOOKED LIKE A PAINTING OF A GREY NUDE. HOURS LATER, HE PAINTED ALONE IN HIS CORNER. IN THE LATE AFTERNOON, WHILE HE WAITED FOR PATRICE, THE SKY TURNED A MOMENTARY BLUE. HADRIAN AND MRS. ITO MET AT THE WHITE RABBIT CAFÉ. THEY SAT AT THE BAR AND DISCUSSED LOUIS'S PAINTINGS AND HOW PATRICE HAD CHANGED THEIR FATES. THEY DRANK TO THE FUTURE. HADRIAN SAID HE WOULD KEEP HIS PORTRAIT, ONLY THE PAINTINGS OF PATRICE WOULD BE SOLD TO THE PATRONESS OF ART TO HANG IN THE MUSEUM. HE WOULD STAY IN NEW YORK AND LIVE IN THE METROPOLITAN. MRS. ITO ASSURED HADRIAN THAT LOUIS LOVED HIM AS MUCH AS A MAN LIKE LOUIS COULD EVER LOVE. MRS. ITO SAID IT WAS IMPORTANT THAT HADRIAN MUST NEVER WAIT TABLES AGAIN, THAT LOUIS HAD ASKED HER TO MAKE SURE THIS WISH OF HIS CAME TRUE. MRS. ITO SAID SHE WOULD RETURN TO JAPAN AND BEGIN HER LIFE OVER AGAIN. THEY RAISED THEIR LAST GLASS OF WINE IN THE AIR AND VOWED EVERY YEAR TO SEE EACH OTHER. THEY SAID GOODBYE TO THE WHITE RABBIT CAFÉ, HELD HANDS, AND WALKED IN THE FALLING SNOW TO THE METROPOLITAN.

She walked circumspectly to The Metropolitan. Her legs traversed the virgin snow, her footsteps engraved wells of white, leaving a trail of her existence in the flanks of the city's bodily morning galaxy. She heard the plural syllables of migratory birds fleeing the starkness and lusterless cold. It was full winter, their ninth year together, and a gelatinous band of slate-blue intersected the sky so far away from the tallest building so distant from modern time.

Patrice removed her wet shoes and socks and carried them in her hands as she walked up the stairs. Her toes gripped the wood in a way she had never experienced before, as if at any time she might breathe too hard or not at all, and lose her balance and tumble to the bottom of the stairs lying there for hours, dying.

She entered the room and slowly stripped her body of clothes and sank despairingly into the red velvet couch. She dug her hand into the crack of the pillows. Minutes passed without words. Louis stood in the corner with cigarette hanging from his lips, and she ebbed alongside his dolorous airs. She inhaled and she swallowed and her heart murmured its wintery hibernatory sigh.

Outside his window, a fish-colored world gleamed wetness and caught
living material dredged in nets. A thatched web of ropes tied and twined
with slaverous hands in need of food. A twisted parable of winter's lure,
the promise of unhungered madness and reasoning in the swell of
whispering snow falling and falling.

She poised herself like a small whisper in a loud room of art. It was ruinous
how he stood in his corner still desirous of art. It was ruinous and ruthless
all the while she sank farther and farther into the red velvet. The grandfather
clock chimed six o'clock and his paintbrush twirled and stoked a mound of
blue, periods of punctuation, a pause and a pause and a pause.
"Look at me," he said.

Her patience was immense. Her eyes moved with deftness. She looked
at the folds of his white shirt, the creases in his pants, and the unpolished
leather of his shoes, tarnished from days spent pacing the hardwood floor.
When their eyes finally met a smile spread across his sea of a face.
She watched his paintbrush fly through the air, and blue splattered his canvas
as the snow outside his window thickened and multiplied into an endless
flush of pure white.

"This is all we have left to care for." She clasped her hands across her chest
as if immersed in an introspective moment of time when a woman sees
she is with another and yet she is singularly alone.

She felt immeasurably aged, her feet now dry and her throat parched.
A small quadrant of youth clung to her heartbeat, an innocent tremor
pulsated from her fingers she kept hidden in the crevices of the pillows.
It was time, time for him to scumble her portrait with immortality's loss,
to instill her with the human qualities of death.

"Artists never really finish their work," she whispered. "They abandon
their work. That's the terrible truth. The more one works on a painting,
the more it becomes impossible to finish it."

She drifted and circumscribed her essence in the molecular magnificent dust
that surfaced between them, the sorrow and the pity and the unrequited
passion. Her hand ran along the selvage of the red velvet couch.
It was enough. The time had come for enough.
All that mattered was enough. They had had nine years of enough.

She slowly touched the softness, and her finger-ends dug into the velvet,
burrowing herself into the tiniest of holes, willing their fabled world to end.

The two legs of his easel still stood on the black marks he had painted
on the hardwood floor. The city outside his window grew fainter and fainter.
Nothing could molest them.

She placed her palm on her heart. "This is all we have left to leave in
this world. You must stop before the snow disappears."

Spellbound by his last color of blue, she reached her fingers into the crack
of the pillows and pulled out the glass phial. She removed her hand
as if she were emptying a great reservoir. She opened the lid.
The room filled with the smell of bitter almonds.
She studied the contents with the eyes of ennui.
She poured the oil in a glass and walked to the corner.
She pressed her lips to the window, and she breathed in and out.
Moisture spread and disappeared.

Patches of light on the Brooklyn Bridge caught his eyes. "One more minute,"
Louis begged. "One more minute with this light."

Each drawn breath only a momentary refuge, he painted incisive strokes
of blue plums. The air simmered the benighted hour of lightness
and darkness, and he smeared streaks of blue in the wet cones of her lips.
Strangely, he felt it impossible to paint what he saw. The angles of her cheeks
shone like lone stars, a face applauding its own pigments. Her hair curled
fetchingly away from her cheekbones, and with his fingernail he scrabbled
blue in the well of her eyes. He had a little sorrow. He imagined Hadrian and
Mrs. Ito walking together in the falling snow. He swelled Patrice's eyes with
the acid bath of truth. His paintbrush hovered like a benevolent cloud over
her, his wrist tremored as life outside his window pulsated night's savaged
beauty, city feet returning a somber gait home.

They stayed like this for many minutes. The grandfather clock chimed
the half-hour. Strangely, too, she waited for him to remove the glass
from her hand to drink the liquid and slowly die.

BOOK FOUR

Spring

43. *Spring* 1949

TWIN BROTHERS SLEEP, AND DEATH SET LOUIS DOWN IN THE METROPOLITAN
AND FLEW THROUGH THE CRACKS. EVEN IN HIS DEATH, HE FOUND ALL OF IT
READY BEFORE HIM, HIS PAINTBRUSHES AND TIN TUBES OF PAINT PRECISELY
LINED IN A ROW, HIS CLEAN WHITE RAGS, AND HIS THREE-LEGGED EASEL WAITING
IN THE CORNER FOR HIS REFLECTION TO APPEAR IN THE EMPTY WHITE CANVAS
PERCHED ON THE LIP. EVEN IN HIS DEATH, HADRIAN AND PATRICE KEPT HIS
THINGS IN PLACE AS HE HAD WISHED.

Down from under the clouds, Louis looked at the room with eyes of
a dead man in the ether of neither here nor there. He inhaled Patrice's
scent, tasted her ocean of flesh. They roused each other. They remained
silent and touched the hollows of flesh with tender fingers only known
to suffering comrades unafraid of the splendors of death.

He husbanded the room. He reclaimed his walls and hardwood floor,
prolonged his time like a symphony of memories longing to last forever.
He telescoped the room looking for unwelcome persons. He saw the pigeons
outside his window still begging for bread, the Brooklyn Bridge still standing
like a prehistoric animal, the fountain of nymphs still spouting her waterfalls,
the antique grandfather clock still existing side by side modern time.

Patrice lay on the red velvet couch and watched him move through the room.
She sank her chin on her breastbone and licked her lips. "There is not much
time. I can only give you one day worth all the rest." She held out her hand.
"Time is the atmosphere we breathe."

There was a stir in the room, and they slipped together through the cracks
in the wall and flew. He followed her into a deep sea, leaving his manhood
behind in the wake. He held her by the waist, and she became woven linen
on his arm. Bound together, full of the soft coloring of familiar understanding
in the throes of time fletched with death, they traversed the city deep in the
rapture of sleep.

The museum doors were locked. They entered the hallowed wealthy halls.
The early morning chambered love of art greeted Louis in a way that never
existed before.

"Nothing in art is to be despised." Patrice reached out her hand. She restored

lost movement. They strolled together through the museum. She held him
close, guided him with motherly hands consumed by the desire to save his
youth. She was singularly innocent as she escorted him to the East wing
where the paintings of her he had painted were hanging on the white walls.
Their affliction thinking themselves quite forgotten disappeared.

She handed him a paintbrush and stepped back.

Four immediacies overcame him in the early morning infatuation with art.
He was eager to look on his own paintings with pure eyes.
He wished to purge and rid his serpents of ignorance and hate.
When he moved, there were no shadows.
Franz stood next to him proud of the outcome.

Louis held the wood between his fingers, forming the most dangerous relationship
in the world, and he mated with color's passion. He dipped the bristles in red
and inched closer to her portrait, dabbed her open mouth with a more steady hand
of a dead man that now held the mystical hue of red sieved by time, a hue void of
troubles and fear. He laced her mouth with delicate red, stretched and smoothed
her tongue, and pointed a glint of rubies along the contours of her open lips.
Gravity pulled him down from her mouth to her neck where he clasped
his newfound hue to her throat. With the flat of his hand he rubbed her flesh,
fattened her neck with the neglected words he had forgotten to say.
Her veins swelled with the color of forgiveness, her face turned that corner,
the kinetic beauty of a being whose majestic soul became what all humans dreamed.
Even in his death living for this one day, seeing his art hanging in the museum,
the flush and fire of triumph reigned.

Patrice gave him this time. Even in his death he painted her in
silence, the sleeping sinews of her flesh and her quiet bones.
He found the most brilliant hue of red and she watched him add
jewels around her mouth. She watched his paintbrush sweep across
her landscape as if he were cleansing her body of terror and shame,
years of venom and captivity.

A rare sensation invaded her, the bare bones of being mortal, a vulnerability
as the little life still in her slowly left. She sat down on the wood bench
to preserve the small speck of life in her.

The end closed in. She felt a queer mixture of feelings. The East wing

resonated with the purr of art, and his dead body played with the whims
of the early morning hours, as if he were in plenty of time.

The unknown awaited for her and she smiled. Louis blew her a spring kiss.
She longed to stay, but the stabbings of reality pulled her. She looked at her
portraits for the last time and she breathed enormous strength in the dead
painter and she turned from him and left his art behind. She walked away
from the paintings and out of the museum, her carriage polite conciliation.

Early morning white dew speckled the pavement. A few strangers on the
streets faintly malign. The colorless drama and the insubstantial air kept
her committed to a gentle gait. She was left alone to wander up and down
the avenues and streets.

She trembled on the edge and held to herself, every part of her tightening
to the hold. She waded through the city with no destination in mind.

She saw herself in the laps of her gods in the ocean stream that held earth
in place. She had defied her gods but she would find rest. She would sleep
deep in dream. She would no longer guard the secrets, nor smell his
turpentine-infested room, nor inhale his cigarette smoke, nor hear the
elusive chimes of the grandfather clock, nor lie naked on a red velvet
couch, forever without. He had waited to paint the finest and most
extraordinary red hue in his death, and she, too, had waited to instill
him with her grandeur and riches until the end, in the caverns of art.

Being on the verge, she took her leave. Drawn toward the river, she turned
the final corner and she witnessed the last ray of light warm her flesh,
broken shrouds of pewter mist sifted her bare shoulders, and more life
breath slipped away, one breath at a time in the city of the Americas,
in blossoming spring, the time of year the sun flowered earth open,
the sorrowful and melancholic birth of flower petals opened and an
implosion of fragrances exploded, and the remnants of the war, the ashes,
the bones, and the lilies-of-the-field, bathed in the effervescent light.

Age brushed her throat.
She probed her heart
for the conversation with the artist,
for the mad colorings of sorrow
in the lost moments of art.

New York City opened her doors and the going and coming, the city's
obsessive rhythms pulsated life. Strangers in twos and threes and
solitaires were swimming upstream, her breath dim and faint alongside
the yawning gulf of the sea.

And then she heard the hush of rain, the small sound clouding the city,
the cry of spring. She felt it all anew, a spring in the heart of everyone
and everything in the aftermath of the war, and the young seaside girls
in her thoughts, their naked innocence spilled from the sky and sprinkled
the city with spring's warmth.

The maturity of experience that ages a woman filled her lungs
as she breathed the last airs of death gently pulsing her throat.

She was remembered. Her pace quickened and her gait straddled the
avenues and streets and she searched for a place to lie down and die.
She was remembered.
She would be seen in the East wing of the museum for five hundred years
more, her portrait, her anatomy, the inside of her heart and her soul no
longer hidden from view.
She glided past and through humans, and her veins opened, seething
the beauty of her art in the minds that lay dormant in everyone.
She kneeled in the reeds by the river and authored her own death.
The Brooklyn Bridge towered in the horizon like an escort from world
to world.

Her lips parted, "I am still alive," and her face turned that corner
of death's smile.
Even in death, she lay in horizontal silence.

THE END

ACKNOWLEDGMENTS

Jack Remick invited me to Third Sunday and I brought pages of *Patrice* that were workshopped by some of the finest writers / poets / visual artists in Seattle. I'm grateful to Irene Drennan, Jo Nelson, Priscilla Long, Gordon Wood, M. Anne Sweet, Francia Recalde, Jim Karnitz, Joel Chafetz, Don Harmon, Carol Ovenburg, Matt Rizzo, and, of course, Jack Remick. Their meticulous readings of my work followed by constructive feedback always enhanced and added polish to my words. During my dark writerly moments, Irene Drennan, Priscilla Long, Jack Remick, Gordon Wood, and M. Anne Sweet pulled me out from the depths—pushed me to keep creating work.

For many years, Robert Ray gave me guidance during writing practice at Tio's / Louisa's on Friday afternoons. I thank Robert Ray for teaching me to stay committed to writing, to stay with my voice.

Every Sunday I write with a group of women, who add a different patina to my work—writing practice and a trusting place of expression. I want to thank Sandra E. Jones, Stacy Lawson, Susan Knox, Janet Yoder, Carol Bolt, Billie Condon, Pam Carter, Arleen Williams, and Ella Andrews for their continued willingness to travel along with me via words. Their support buoys me.

My family and friends have supported my writing habit (my passion) by letting me steal time away from them to find that alone place to write. It takes a community to keep me on course, and the following have either reined me in or inspired me: PK, Patricia Gale, Jaclynn Hiranaka, Gary Gale, Kymberly Gale, Andrew Gale, Greg Gale, Mark Gale, Janice Kunitsugu, Scott Parducci, Deborah Pursifull, Lori DeMarre, Elisa Gonzalez, Joaquin Gonzalez, Leah Elgin, Winnie Alston, Amy Doerzbacher, Josie Zhuo, Yang Dan, Dee Paiement, Amy Davis, Hitomi Sawabe, Sue Mings, Phileo Alexander, Rona Frances, Heidi Petry, Leslie Kim, Helen Fitzpatrick, Susi Rosenthal, Takako Aikawa, Flora Ramírez-Bustamante, Joseph Pentheroudakis, Miki Suzuki, Melissa Bertocchini, Sandy Poliachik, Stewart Stern, Wendy Lippmann, Sharilyn Carroll, Rivy Pouplo Kletenik, Bill Pennington, Carole Hurst, Michael Mendonsa, Racelle Bustrup, Jen Picken, Stephanie Vandenack, Ethan Johnson, Sarah Bergey, Francesca Merlini, Omar Curiel, TJ Hatfield, Steve Murray, Andy Brawner, and Dennis O'Reilly.

I always turn to artist / designer Pamela Farrington to shape my words into a visual form. She adds an artistry that transforms a sea of black typeface into atmospheric stardust. velvetdesignstudio.com

Anne Moreau is a steward of language—she is precise, thoughtful, and approaches the complexities of words with wonderment. She proofread this book with careful eyes. annemoreau.com

Lori Mahoney added the final touches that made many parts whole.

ABOUT THE AUTHOR

Geri Gale is a poet and writer of prose. This particular book reveals her hybrid style of writing. She lives in Seattle and is in a constant state of creating a body of work. Gale is the author of *Waiting*. Her poetry and prose have appeared in numerous publications. For more details about past and future works, visit gerigale.com.

NOTES

It took me six years to write this book. I started writing *Patrice* in 2000. The story morphed into an art form—a poemella—as my heroine Patrice came to life, and the world of art and the interiority of women unlayered as Louis added more layers of paint to the canvas. It took everything out of me not to change the story into a more traditional story. I worked hard to reveal the atmospheric dialogue between the muse and the painter.

Louis creates twenty-four paintings of Patrice in this book. As I write these words in 2013, I often wonder if one day an artist reading *Patrice: a poemella* will feel inspired to paint what Louis saw. If you create a painting of Patrice that Louis painted in this book, contact gerigale.com.

The Brooklyn Bridge is my favorite bridge. As a child, I was a passenger in my mother's car driving across it many times. I hope one day to walk across it.

In 2008 I met Josie Zhuo and began acupuncture treatments. I was terribly afraid of all medicinal needles. She cured me of my shoulder pain and taught me lessons about compassion, letting go, seeking a smooth and balanced life, and building a solid foundation in this life for my death-journey to the world to come. Mrs. Ito, Louis's acupuncturist, came to me three years earlier.

CREDITS

Patrice: a poemella was awarded honorable mention in the 2009 Leapfrog Press Fiction Contest.

The words that Patrice whispers to Louis in chapter "42. Winter 1948," are from James Lord's *A Giacometti Portrait*:
  "That's the terrible thing: the more one works on a picture,
  the more impossible it becomes to finish it."

The definition of a poemella that appears at the beginning of this book was written by Geri Gale.

PRAISE FOR *PATRICE: A POEMELLA*

An intense, sumptuous prose-poetry exploration of inspiration, sacrifice and art.

With uninhibited brush strokes, Gale's impassioned debut offers an extended, self-reflexive allegory of artistic abnegation and creation. The author marries the characterization of prose to the sensuality and linguistic precision of poetry in a form she dubs a "poemella."

A baroque, sensual tour de force that elevates art above all else.
  —*Kirkus Reviews*

Geri Gale's *Patrice: a poemella* is obsessive, luscious, delicious. It invites you into the river of language and carries you to the heart of what it means to make art, to be an artist, to be an artist's muse. *Patrice* is timeless and it is mesmerizing.
  —Priscilla Long
    poet, writer of essays, fiction, history & science
    author of *The Writer's Portable Mentor: A Guide to Art, Craft, and the Writing Life; Where the Sun Never Shines: A History of America's Bloody Coal Industry;* and *Crossing Over*
    priscillalong.com

In *Patrice* you get to watch a writer fuse the intense poetic line with the extended narrative line to create a new form. Geri Gale calls this a poemella— by this she intends to fuse a poem with its compressed imagery to a novella with its complicated story line. In effect, this is a modern epic. This poemella is written in a new language that jams together words which, until Gale fits them into her images, have not been fused before.

It's not every day that we stand witness to the creation of a new form—in *Patrice* you get to see evolution and creation at work.
  —Jack Remick
    poet, novelist & screenwriter
    author of *The Book of Changes, The Deification, Gabriela and the Widow, Blood,* and *Satori*
    jackremick.com

From her first words, the poetics of this transformative work take you on a wonderful creative journey. Unlike any other offerings of literary imagination I've digested, *Patrice* is an intimate, sensuous and historical encounter with the creative process of souls merging through art, with all its simple joys woven in with the intimate struggle entailed. This is achieved by delving beyond the surfaces of appearances and into the depths of seeking the mystery and meaning of existence through patient dialogue between a muse and painter.

> —Gordon Wood, painter
> Gordon H. Wood Art & Design
> gordonwoodart.com

Geri Gale's poemella—a novella executed in exquisitely turned poetic lines— is breathtaking in its emotion, power, and artistry. Although seemingly implausible, the existence of this 500-year-old woman, Patrice, is never in doubt. Her sensuality opens the painter's body and soul. Gale's understanding of the painter's studio, brushstrokes, color, and technique brings to life the intimacy of the painter / model relationship, and the reader is drawn into a world that is immediate and real.

> —M. Anne Sweet, poet & artist
> author of *Nailed to the Sky* and several graphic poems
> studiosixeight.com

In this sumptuous book, *Patrice: a poemella,* Geri Gale offers a rich, rewarding literary feast of imaginative, luscious language and story: mythologies of art, longing, place and being, set within the historical context of a terrible war, and a great city. A book to be savored slowly, over a glass of red wine, on a red velvet divan. Lovely. Lyrical. A treasure.

> —Deborah Pursifull, poet

There's a lavish richness to Gale's writing that flows through her enchanting unmasking of what it is to be an artist's muse. In her expertly woven tale of wartime, an indelible story of passion flourishes in swathes of greed, purity, and paint. A book to be savored, word by delicious word.

> —TJ Hatfield, copywriter

I take her work out like I would a snifter of Grand Marnier and sip it because it's so rich, aromatic, and the ritual of the amount of drink and the glass that holds it matters.

> —Lori DeMarre, photographer & visual artist

www.ingramcontent.com/pod-product-compliance
Lightning Source LLC
Chambersburg PA
CBHW060647260626
47161CB00008B/3029